"A lot of my rhymes are just to get chuckles out of people. Anybody with half a brain is going to be able to tell when I'm joking and when I'm serious."

– Eminem

"I think the scariest person in the world is the person with no sense of humour."

– Michael J. Fox

CONTENTS

PERFECT DUMP

THIS FIRST RHYME'S GONNA BE FAIRLY SHORT,
AS THERE ISN'T MUCH TO SAY.
ABOUT HOW HAVING THE PERFECT DUMP,
ALWAYS BRIGHTENS MY DAY.

AND IT JUST SORT OF SLIPS OUT,
WITHOUT ANY REAL STRAINING OR GRIPING.
AND THEN THE JOY IS SOON COMPLETED,
WITH THE MINIMUM OF WIPING.

BUT IT'S NOT JUST THE LACK OF FUSS,
WHICH MAKES ME FEEL SO GREAT.
AS IT'S ABOUT HAVING THE SENSATION, TOO,
THAT I'VE GENUINELY LOST WEIGHT.

AND THEN I HAPPILY LEAVE THE CRAPPER,
WITH A BIG GRIN ON MY UGLY MUG.
BECAUSE I'M FEELING THAT MUCH LIGHTER,
AND EXTREMELY SELF-SATISFIED AND SMUG!

BODY ODOUR

WE ALL EMIT A PERSONAL ODOUR,
WHICH OTHERS CAN SMELL.
THOUGH, IN MOST IT'S SO FAINT,
WE CAN BARELY EVEN TELL.

BUT THAT'S NOT SO WITH ME, UNFORTUNATELY,
AS MY B.O. REALLY STINKS.
AN AROMA SO PUNGENT,
IT CAN'T BE HIDDEN WITH *LYNX*.

AND I SWEAT THROUGH MY CLOTHES,
EVEN WHEN IT'S NOT THAT HOT.
CREATING UNSIGHTLY PATCHES OF DAMP,
WHICH SMELL MORE LIKE ROT.

AND MY ARMPITS ARE ALWAYS FLOWING,
LIKE A RIVER THAT'S BURST ITS BANKS.
PRODUCING A SCENT SO LETHAL,
IT DAREN'T BE USED IN THE WORST PRANKS.

AND I'VE TRIED ALL THE CURES, OF COURSE,
BUT WITH VERY LITTLE SUCCESS.
AS THE STENCH OF ROTTING GARBAGE,
IS EXTREMELY HARD TO SUPRESS.

THOUGH, I DID FIND A POWDER ONCE,
WHICH APPEARED TO DO THE TRICK.
BUT IT JUST DIVERTED THE SWEATY PROBLEM,
DOWN TO MY ARSE, BALLS AND DICK!

Irish Bugs:

There once was an Irishwoman from Lusk
who always attracted bugs at dusk.
  The poor dear was called Annie
  and had a rather sweaty fanny
that gave off a really strange musk.

DANDRUFF

NOW, I KNOW WHAT YOU'RE THINKING,
THAT I'M TAKING THE PISS.
BUT DANDRUFF'S SLIGHTLY MEDICAL,
SO MY ARSE YOU CAN KISS.

AND I'M NOT TALKING ABOUT THE MILD CASES,
THE STUFF THAT YOU CAN BARELY SEE.
I'M TALKING ABOUT THE POOR PEOPLE SHEDDING BLIZZARDS,
AND THAT UNLUCKY GROUP INCLUDES ME.

SO, MY HAIR IS JET BLACK,
APART FROM THE STRANDS TURNING GREY.
WHICH HIGHLIGHTS MY DANDRUFF TO THE MAX,
MUCH TO MY CHAGRIN AND DISMAY.

AND IT LOOKS LIKE I'VE BEEN SPRINKLED WITH ICING SUGAR,
OR DUSTED WITH FLOUR.
AND IT UPSETS MY MOJO EVERY DAY,
AND SAPS MY SELF-CONFIDENCE AND POWER.

AND I'VE TRIED ALL THE MEDICATED SHAMPOOS, OF COURSE,
AND EVEN CONSULTED MY GP.
BUT MY SCALP IS STILL ROTTING AWAY,
AND I'M STILL NOT FLAKE FREE.

SO THERE'S NOTHING MORE THAT I CAN DO,
AND I'VE JUST GOT TO LIVE WITH MY PLIGHT.
WHICH IS WHY I'VE CHANGED MY WHOLE WARDROBE,
AND NOW ONLY WEAR WHITE!

Dandruff:

Virginia was a hirsute woman from Cedar Bluff
who had a serious problem with dandruff.
　　She wasn't shedding flakes from her head
　　or her lengthy armpit hair, instead,
but from her disturbingly hairy muff.

KIDNEY STONE

I HAD A KIDNEY STONE ONCE,
AND IT'S THE WORST PAIN I'VE EVER FELT.
SO YOU CAN BELIEVE ME WHEN I SAY,
THIS AIN'T A HEALTH ISSUE YOU WANNA BE DEALT.

AND IT WAS CAUSED BY POOR FLUID INTAKE,
AND THE RESULTING LONG-TERM DEHYDRATION.
WHICH IS SUCH A STUPID THING TO SUFFER FROM,
IN THESE TIMES OF ENLIGHTENED CONTEMPLATION.

BUT I WAS EXTREMELY LUCKY HOWEVER,
AND MANAGED TO PISS THE THING OUT.
ALTHOUGH, IT STILL HURT LIKE A BASTARD,
AND MADE ME SERIOUSLY SHOUT.

AND I LITERALLY SCREAMED MY HEAD OFF,
WHILE IT PASSED THROUGH MY COCK.
AND THEN THE SUDDEN LACK OF PAIN
WAS GENUINELY QUITE A SHOCK.

AND THE STONE WAS ACTUALLY QUITE SMALL,
ONLY THREE TO FOUR MILLIMETRES IN SIZE.
BUT THAT WAS STILL EASILY BIG ENOUGH,
TO SQUEEZE THE TEARS FROM MY EYES.

AND I'M NOT JOKING ABOUT THE PAIN,
WHICH WAS WORSE THAN HAVING A ROOT CANAL DRILLED.
AND THAT'S WHY I NOW DRINK LIKE A FISH,
AND KEEP MY BLADDER CONSTANTLY FILLED!

Fortune-teller:

Madame Zara was a dishonest fortune-teller from Sydney
who was in desperate need of a new kidney.
    She tried conning her gullible client Morgan
    into donating said organ,
but despite her best conniving efforts he didn'ne.

SIDEWAYS PEEING

THE FIRST TIME I MENTIONED THIS WEIRD PHENOMENON,
WAS AT THE END OF MY KINDLE BOOK CALLED: *GUYS*.
THOUGH I DOUBT ANY WOMAN WHO READ IT,
CONSIDERED IT TO BE ANYTHING BUT LIES.

BUT TOILET ACCIDENTS DO HAPPEN, HOWEVER,
NO MATTER HOW HARD A GUY TRIES.
AND WE CAN, VERY OCCASIONALLY,
BE GREETED WITH A RATHER NASTY SURPRISE.

SO, I'LL STEP UP TO THE TOILET LIKE NORMAL,
AND THEN WHIP OUT MY COCK.
BUT INSTEAD OF PEEING RELATIVELY STRAIGHT,
I'LL GET A TERRIBLE SHOCK.

AND IT'S LIKE SOMETHING GETS TWISTED,
OR SNARLED INTO A TANGLE.
AND MY PISS WILL UNEXPECTEDLY SHOOT OUT,
AT A REALLY WEIRD ANGLE.

AND NOW I'M STOOD THERE LIKE AN IDIOT,
CLUTCHING MY POLE.
WHILE I SPRAY STEAMY URINE EVERYWHERE,
EXCEPT INTO THE BOWL.

AND I'M DESPERATELY TRYING TO PEE STRAIGHT,
AND NOT PISS ON THE FLOOR.
BUT MY PLUMBING IS TEMPORARILY SCRAMBLED,
AND MY AIM IS TOO POOR.

AND THIS UNWELCOME EVENT AIN'T SOMETHING
THAT'S JUST PECULIAR TO ME.
AS I'VE DISCUSSED IT WITH ALL MY MATES, TOO,
AND THEY WERE REALLY QUICK TO AGREE.

SO THIS TOILET MISHAP IS QUITE GENUINE,
AND BLOKES WILL OCCASIONALLY MISS.
NOT THAT THAT ABSOLVES THEM, OF COURSE,
FROM CLEANING UP THEIR PUDDLES OF PISS!

GENITAL OCD

NOW, THIS TOPIC MAY NOT BE PLEASANT,
BUT I'M ON A SERIOUS MISSION.
TO FINALLY BRING TO LIGHT,
THIS UNDIAGNOSED MALE CONDITION.

AND I THINK ALL MEN ARE BORN
WITH THIS TERRIBLE, COMPULSIVE AFFLICTION.
WHICH I BELIEVE IS GENUINELY MEDICAL,
AND NOT JUST A SIMPLE ADDICTION.

AND I PERSONALLY TOUCH MY OWN GENITALS
HUNDREDS OF TIMES A DAY.
AND WHEN OR WHERE DOESN'T MATTER,
SO AT WORK, REST OR PLAY.

AND I HONESTLY BELIEVE
THAT THIS IS SOME FORM OF GENITAL OCD.
AND I'M ALSO CONVINCED
THAT IT'S NOT JUST HAPPENING TO ME.

YOU SEE, GUYS HAVE TO HANDLE THEIR GENITALS,
EVERY TIME THEY TAKE A LEAK.
OR WHEN REPOSITIONING FOR COMFORT,
THEY HAVE TO GIVE THEM A TWEAK.

AND WE CAN'T EVEN GET DRESSED
WITHOUT TOUCHING OUR NADS.
AND THEY HAVE TO BE CUPPED DURING SPORT,
AND PROTECTED FROM OTHER LADS.

AND I'LL OFTEN TOUCH MY JUNK RANDOMLY,
JUST TO CHECK IT'S STILL THERE.
WHICH IS SIMILAR TO WHAT WOMEN DO,
WITH THEIR MAKEUP AND HAIR.

AND IT'S A BLOODY GOOD JOB
THAT I WASN'T ALSO BORN WITH TITS.
ELSE, I'D NEED THREE HANDS
JUST TO PLAY WITH ALL MY BITS!

FULL TRAPS

NOTHING INFURIATES ME MORE,
WHEN I'M IN DESPERATE NEED OF A CRAP.
THAN ENTERING THE MEN'S ROOM AT WORK
AND FINDING THERE ISN'T A SINGLE EMPTY TRAP.

AND IF YOU'RE NOT AU FAIT WITH THE TERM TRAP,
THEN THINK, CUBICLE OR STALL.
BUT REGARDLESS OF THE PREFERRED EXPRESSION,
MY BACK'S STILL FIRMLY TO THE WALL.

AND IT'S NOT LIKE NEEDING TO TAKE A PISS,
WHICH I CAN SUPPRESS FOR QUITE A WHILE.
AS I CAN'T DELAY GRAVITY FROM ITS BUSINESS
OF DELIVERING A SMALL, BROWNISH PILE.

SO NOW I HAVE TO WAIT ANXIOUSLY OUTSIDE THE STALLS,
AND TRY NOT TO SHIT MY PANTS.
WHILE I HOPE AND PRAY FOR A SWIFT VACATION,
BY ONE OF THE CUBICLES OCCUPANTS.

AND THE SMALLER THE COMPANY YOU WORK FOR,
THE FEWER THE STALLS THERE ARE.
AND TWO FUCKING CUBICLES FOR FIFTY BLOKES,
IS NEVER GOING TO STRETCH VERY FAR.

ANYWAY, ONCE A TRAP FINALLY BECOMES FREE,
I HAVE TO TAKE WHAT I CAN GET.
WHICH IS USUALLY A SEAT THAT'S STILL WARM,
AND POSSIBLY COVERED IN SWEAT.

AND THERE WILL PROBABLY BE A BAD SMELL, TOO,
WHICH CATCHES IN THE BACK OF MY THROAT.
AND THE LAST USER MAY ALSO HAVE LEFT BEHIND,
A STINKY PRESENT THAT'S STILL AFLOAT.

AND EVEN THOUGH I'VE REACHED CRITICAL MASS,
AND HAVE TO DROP THE KIDS OFF AT THE POOL.
I STILL CHECK THAT THERE'S PLENTY OF TOILET PAPER,
SO I WON'T BE CAUGHT OUT LIKE A FOOL!

XMAS CAROLS

NOW, DON'T GET ME WRONG,
I THINK CHRISTMAS IS GREAT.
EXCEPT FOR FUCKING CAROLS,
WHICH I SERIOUSLY HATE.

AND I DON'T WANT TO DECK THE HALLS,
OR SING AWAY IN A MANGER.
ESPECIALLY OUTSIDE THE HOUSE
OF A COMPLETE FUCKING STRANGER.

SO, I JUST WANT A SILENT NIGHT,
WITHOUT ANY DING DONG MERRILY ON HIGH.
AND IF I HAVE TO HEAR JINGLE BELLS ONCE MORE,
I'LL PROBABLY CRY.

AND THESE AREN'T THE ONLY HYMNS AND CAROLS,
WHICH I THINK ARE SHITTY.
AS THERE'S ALSO THE HOLLY AND THE IVY,
AND ONCE IN ROYAL DAVID'S CITY.

AND SHOULD I EVER CATCH ANY ANNOYING CAROLLERS,
SINGING OUTSIDE OF MY PLACE.
THEN I'LL PUT ASIDE MY FESTIVE SPIRIT,
AND BREAK OUT THE FUCKING MACE!

OUT OF OFFICE

SETTING MY "OUT OF OFFICE" IN OUTLOOK,
JUST BEFORE GOING ON VACATION.
IS ONE OF THOSE VERY SIMPLE PLEASURES,
WHICH BRINGS ME SO MUCH ELATION.

AND THE REASON FOR THIS
IS DOWN TO THE AUTOMATED REPLY.
WHICH HAS A SINISTER CONNOTATION,
THAT'S REALLY HARD TO DENY.

AND I KNOW A POLITE EMAIL WILL BE GENERATED,
AND RETURNED TO THE SENDER.
BUT WHAT IT'S REALLY IMPLYING IS,
"SCREW YOU, ARSEHOLE! I'M AWAY ON A BENDER!"

MISFORTUNE

I'M REFERRING TO OTHER PEOPLES, OF COURSE!
I MEAN, WHAT DID YOU THINK?
THAT MY OWN PERSONAL MISFORTUNES
WOULD BE TICKLING ME PINK.

AND I KNOW THERE'S A LIMIT, OF COURSE,
AND I HAVE TO DRAW A LINE.
BUT I FIGURE, SO LONG AS NOBODY DIES,
THEN EVERYTHING'S FINE.

AND I CAN'T BE THE ONLY ONE WHO GIGGLES,
AT OTHER PEOPLES' SUFFERING.
AS ALL THE STUFF UPLOADED TO *YOUTUBE*,
IS UNDER CONSTANT STRAIN AND BUFFERING.

AND THEN THERE'S *RUDE TUBE*, OF COURSE,
WHICH CHERRY-PICKS THE BEST CLIPS.
THAT SHOWCASE PEOPLES' STUPID BEHAVIOUR,
AND HILARIOUS DIGNITY SLIPS.

AND PEOPLE ARE STILL HAPPILY CREATING NEW CLIPS,
EVERY DAY OF THE YEAR.
WHICH KEEPS ME LAUGHING MY ARSE OFF,
AND MY CONSCIENCE FAIRLY CLEAR.

AND THEY WOULDN'T KEEP SHOOTING THIS STUFF,
IF THEY DIDN'T WANT US TO WATCH.
AND WHO DOESN'T CRACK A SLY SMILE,
WHEN SOME WANNABE STUNTMAN KNACKERS HIS CROTCH!

Professional Skateboarder:

There was a professional skateboarder called Finn
who entered a national contest to win.
　　But during his best trick
　　he damaged his dick
and then he split open his chin.

OLD AGE

BEING A PENSIONER SUCKS,
AND WE GET NO RESPECT.
AS WE WOBBLE DOWN THE STREET,
BARELY ERECT.

AND WE'VE GOT CREAKING JOINTS,
AND SOME BRITTLE BONES.
BUT THAT'S PRETTY TAME
COMPARED TO OUR KIDNEY STONES.

AND WE'RE ALSO LOSING OUR HEARING,
AND LOSING OUR SIGHT.
AND THE LEAST UNEXPECTED THING,
NOW GIVES US A FRIGHT.

PLUS, WE SLEEP MORE DURING THE DAY,
THAN WE DO AT NIGHT.
AND WE'RE ALSO STEADILY LOSING,
OUR VERACIOUS APPETITE.

AND WE ALSO GO TO MORE FUNERALS NOW,
THAN WE DID IN THE PAST.
AS WE'RE BURYING OUR OLD FRIENDS,
SO WE COULD WELL END UP BEING THE LAST.

AND WE'RE HAVING TROUBLE WITH OUR FACULTIES,
WHICH HAVE NEARLY ALL GONE.
WHICH IS WHY THE TV VOLUME'S TURNED TO A HUNDRED,
AND THE SUBTITLES ARE ON.

AND WE'VE GOT A TOUCH OF ARTHRITIS, TOO,
AND A SLIGHTLY DODGY HEART.
AND WE CAN NO LONGER TRUST OURSELVES,
TO LET LOOSE A FART.

THEN THERE'RE THE OUTBURSTS OF SWEARING,
AND OUR CRAZY ELDERLY RANTS.
NOT TO MENTION SUFFERING THE HUMILIATION
OF WEARING INCONTINENCE PANTS!

THE INTERNET

THE INTERNET HAS CHANGED OUR LIVES,
AND I'D SAY MOSTLY FOR THE BETTER.
BUT DESPITE INCREASING OUR WAYS OF STAYING IN TOUCH,
IT'S KILLED THE HUMBLE LETTER.

NOW, I KNOW THIS IS A MASSIVE SUBJECT,
AND WAY TOO MUCH FOR ONE SHORT RHYME.
SO WE'LL JUST STICK WITH THE MORE FUN STUFF,
AND LEAVE THE REST FOR ANOTHER TIME.

AND SPEAKING OF COMMUNICATING,
WE'VE GOT EMAIL, CHATROOMS AND LOTS OF SOCIAL MEDIA.
AND FOR READING UP ON LITERALLY ANY SUBJECT,
THERE'S A SITE CALLED *WIKIPEDIA*.

WE CAN ALSO SEARCH FOR PORN, OF COURSE,
FOR THE PURPOSES OF MONKEY SPANKING.
AND THEN WE CAN COMPARE OUR CAR INSURANCE,
AND DO SOME ONLINE BANKING.

AND WE CAN VISIT *YOUTUBE* FOR AMUSING VIDEOS,
AND *AMAZON* FOR BUYING ANYTHING SEEN OR WRITTEN.
AND THEN WE CAN USE THAT FAMOUS SEARCH ENGINE,
FOR FINDING LOL PICS OF THE CUTE *SNIPER KITTEN*.

AND *GOOGLE* SUPPLIES US WITH MAPS FOR FINDING PLACES,
ALONG WITH THE DETAILED *STREET VIEW*.
WHICH IS REALLY FUN TO PLAY WITH,
WHEN WE'VE GOT SOME WORK WE DON'T WANT TO DO.

AND WHAT OF SHOPPING AND DATING, THEN,
AND BOOKING ALL OF OUR HOLIDAYS?
AS WE'RE SO USED TO DOING IT ONLINE NOW,
THAT WE'VE FORGOTTEN THE PREVIOUS WAYS.

THEN THERE'S KEEPING TRACK OF ALL THE NEWS AND SPORT,
AND GENERAL ENTERTAINMENT.
THAT MAKES US EASILY LOSE TRACK OF TIME,
AND LEAVES US WONDERING WHERE IT WENT.

AND THERE'S JUST TIME TO MENTION GAMBLING,
WITH LOTS OF SLOTS AND MANY FORMS OF BINGO.
PLUS, THERE'S PLAYING ONLINE POKER,
WHERE IT HELPS TO KNOW THE STATS AND LINGO.

AND WE CAN EVEN DELVE INTO OUR HISTORY NOW,
AND BUILD A PERSONAL FAMILY TREE.
BUT UNLIKE MANY THINGS ON THE INTERNET,
THIS PARTICULAR SERVICE ISN'T FREE!

DRUNK TYPES

NOW, WE ALL KNOW THAT GETTING DRUNK
SERIOUSLY AFFECTS HOW WE ACT.
BUT THERE ARE ONLY FOUR TYPES OF DRUNKEN PEOPLE,
AND THAT'S JUST A FACT.

SO I'M GOING TO LIST THE FOUR CATEGORIES,
AND THEN GIVE YOU A QUICK GUIDE.
AND THE TYPES ARE HEMMINGWAY, NUTTY PROFESSOR,
MARY POPPINS AND MR. HYDE.

SO LET'S START WITH THE HEMMINGWAY CATEGORY,
OUT OF LITERARY RESPECT.
WHERE THE DRINKERS SEE VERY LITTLE DECREASE,
IN THEIR CONSCIENTIOUSNESS OR INTELLECT.

AND THEY REMAIN EXTREMELY RELIABLE,
IN SPITE OF ALL THE DRUNKEN HYPE.
AND ROUGHLY FOUR IN EVERY TEN PEOPLE,
FALL IN TO THIS PARTICULAR TYPE.

BUT IT'S ONLY ONE OF FIVE DRUNKS,
WHO LAND IN THE NUTTY PROFESSOR CATEGORY.
AND I'M QUITE HAPPY TO ADMIT TO YOU,
THAT ONE OF THOSE PEOPLE IS ME.

AND IT'S FULL OF INTROVERTS WHO BECOME EXTROVERTS,
THE MORE THAT THEY DRINK.
AND I'VE BEEN KNOWN TO STRIP OFF MY CLOTHES,
BEFORE PUKING IN THE SINK.

SO THE MARY POPPINS TYPE IS NEXT,
AND INCLUDES FAR MORE WOMEN THAN GUYS.
BUT, GIVEN THEY GET SWEETER THE MORE THEY DRINK,
THAT'S HARDLY A SURPRISE.

BUT THEY'RE NOT ALL NICE DRUNKS, THOUGH,
AND SOME TURN INTO REAL PSYCHOBITCHES.
WHICH IS WHY THE ERs ARE OCCASIONALLY FULL
OF DRUNKEN WOMEN WHO NEED STITCHES.

SO THE MR. HYDE GROUP IS LAST, THEN,
AND IT'S FULL OF DRUNKS TO BE DETESTED.
AS THEY ARE THE MOST LIKELY SET OF PEOPLE
TO BLACKOUT OR GET ARRESTED.

AND ALTHOUGH IT CAN BE DANGEROUS
TO WATCH THESE IDIOTS GET PISSED.
IT'S STILL NOT THE SORT OF FUN SIGHT
THAT SHOULD GENERALLY BE MISSED!

"BRO"

NOW, ACCORDING TO DAVID CAMERON,
BARACK OBAMA CALLS HIM "BRO".
THOUGH WHAT OBAMA REALLY MEANS BY THIS,
I DON'T EXACTLY KNOW.

AND THERE ARE TWO MEANINGS FOR "BRO",
WHICH I'LL QUICKLY DISCUSS.
THOUGH, GIVEN THE SIZE OF THIS TINY STORY,
IT'S HARDLY WORTH THE FUSS.

SO, THE FIRST MEANING IS OBVIOUS,
AS "BRO" IS SHORT FOR BROTHER.
AND IS USED AS A TERM OF ENDEARMENT,
REGARDLESS OF SHARING THE SAME MOTHER.

AND THIS IS THE CONTEXT, OF COURSE,
THAT CAMERON BELIEVES OBAMA IS USING.
BUT IT COULD BE THE SECOND ONE, THOUGH,
WHICH IS MUCH MORE AMUSING.

SO, THE SECOND CONTEXT IS "ALPHA-MALE IDIOT",
LIKE FRAT BOYS GETTING DRUNK.
WHICH WOULD INDICATE THAT OBAMA THINKS
THAT DAVID CAMERON'S A PUNK.

AND THIS IS AN INSULT, OF COURSE,
AND GENERATED CONFUSION IN THE BRITISH PRESS.
AS THE FIRST CONTEXT IS VERY GOOD,
BUT THE SECOND ONE IS A MESS.

HOWEVER, THERE IS A THIRD OPTION,
THAT WOULD EXPLAIN WHY OBAMA'S USING "BRO".
WHICH I BELIEVE IS THE CORRECT ONE,
EVEN THOUGH I'M OBVIOUSLY NOT IN THE KNOW.

AND I THINK OBAMA'S REALLY USING THE TERM "BRO",
BECAUSE HE CAN'T REMEMBER CAMERON'S NAME.
BUT THEN, THE PRIME MINISTER'S NOT ALL THAT MEMORABLE,
SO THE PRESIDENT'S HARDLY TO BLAME!

BAD HABITS

I'VE ACTUALLY GOT MANY BAD HABITS,
BUT WE'LL START WITH MY PROLIFIC SWEARING.
WHICH BRINGS ME, NOT UNSURPRISINGLY,
AN AWFUL LOT OF UNAMUSED GLARING.

AND I COMPLETELY UNDERSTAND, OF COURSE,
THAT IT'S NOT A VERY CLEVER THING TO DO.
BUT I JUST DON'T GIVE A FLYING FUCK,
SO LET'S MOVE ON TO BAD HABIT NUMBER TWO.

SO BITING MY FINGERNAILS IS NEXT,
WHICH IS VERY UNPLEASANT TO SEE.
AND I'VE TRIED REALLY HARD TO STOP,
BUT THE SOLUTION'S COMPLETELY BEYOND ME.

AND I GUESS THE PROBLEM'S WITH MY WILLPOWER,
WHICH JUST ISN'T STRONG ENOUGH.
AND NEITHER WERE ALL THE CURES I TRIED,
NOT EVEN PAINTING ON THAT FOUL-TASTING STUFF.

SO LET'S MOVE ON TO PICKING MY NOSE, THEN,
WHICH NEVER GETS OLD.
AND I LIKE TO CRAM MY LITTLE FINGER RIGHT UP THERE,
LIKE I'M DIGGING FOR GOLD.

NOT THAT THE STUFF I EXTRACT IS GOLD, OF COURSE,
IT'S MORE OF A PALE, YELLOW GREEN.
BUT I STILL HAPPILY EAT IT, MIND YOU,
WHICH IS DISTURBINGLY CHILDISH AND OBSCENE.

SO WE'RE PAST HALFWAY NOW,
AND MY AWFUL HABIT OF FARTING IS NEXT.
ALTHOUGH, I AM SECRETLY WONDERING
IF YOU'RE STILL READING AND ENJOYING THIS TEXT.

BUT I'M SURE THAT YOU ARE, THOUGH,
AS WE OBVIOUSLY SHARE THE SAME SENSE OF HUMOUR.
AND MY TOXIC FARTS ARE SILENT AND DEADLY,
THE GASEOUS EQUIVALENT OF A PUMA.

SO MY BURPING IS OUR NEXT TOPIC,
ALTHOUGH, MAYBE THAT SHOULD BE BELCHING.
BUT WHICHEVER TERM YOU PREFER,
IT'S EXACTLY THE SAME THING.

AND MY BURPS ARE VERY LOUD,
AND EARN ME LOTS OF ACCUSATORY LOOKS.
BUT I SIMPLY IGNORE THE OTHER LIBRARY USERS,
AND JUST KEEP ON READING MY BOOKS.

AND I ALSO SNEEZE A HELLUVA LOT, TOO,
AND NEVER COVER MY NOSE OR MOUTH.
BECAUSE I WAS DRAGGED UP IN A BARN,
IN THE COUNTRYSIDE DOWN SOUTH.

AND IF YOU THINK THAT THAT'S BAD,
THEN THE WORST IS STILL YET TO COME.
AS I'M OVER FORTY YEARS OLD NOW
AND STILL SUCKING MY THUMB!

The Accused:

The accused shuffled into the courtroom half-hearted
and waited for proceedings to get started.
    Then the judge hurried in,
    demanded complete silence to begin,
and out of the blue he unexpectedly farted.

BIRTHMARK

I'VE GOT A BIRTHMARK ON MY RIGHT ARSE CHEEK
SHAPED LIKE A PENGUIN TAKING A DUMP.
BUT I HARDLY EVER SEE IT, THOUGH,
SO IT DOESN'T GIVE ME THE HUMP.

AND WHEN YOU ACTUALLY THINK ABOUT IT,
IT'S DEFINITELY IN THE RIGHT PLACE.
AS I'D RATHER HAVE IT DOWN THERE,
THAN STUCK ON MY BLOODY FACE!

Mole:

Nathaniel noticed a new and rather dark mole
that'd appeared on the shaft of his pole.
    He was obviously worried about skin cancer,
    but still avoided seeking an answer
from his cute doctor whose name was Nicole.

29

JIZZ SOCK

I'VE SEEN AMERICAN COMEDIANS ON THE TELLY
REFER TO THIS PHENOMENON NUMEROUS TIMES.
WHICH IS WHY I'VE DECIDED TO COVER IT
IN ONE OF MY RHYMES.

AND I JUST CAN'T IMAGINE WHY,
WHEN A GUY'S MILKING HIS COCK.
THAT HE'D IGNORE A PLENTIFUL SUPPLY OF TOILET PAPER,
AND INSTEAD REACH FOR A SOCK.

AND I'VE GIVEN THIS A LOT OF THOUGHT, MIND YOU,
AND HAVE SOME MAJOR CONCERNS.
WHICH MOSTLY REVOLVE AROUND THE WORRY
OF GETTING SERIOUS FRICTION BURNS.

AND THEN, WHAT IF YOU FORGOT TO WASH THE SOCK
BEFORE YOU PUT IT BACK ON YOUR FEET?
AS THAT'S NOT THE SORT OF PERSONAL EVENT,
WHICH WOULD GENERATE A FUN TWEET.

AND IS THIS JUST AN AMERICAN TRAIT,
OR DO MEN FROM OTHER NATIONS DO IT AS WELL?
BUT I DOUBT I'LL EVER FIND OUT, THOUGH,
AS I CAN'T IMAGINE ANYONE WILL TELL.

AND PERHAPS IT'S IN MY BEST INTEREST,
NOT TO ACTUALLY CONDUCT A POLL.
AS I COULD BE THE ONLY GUY ON THE PLANET,
JERKING OFF INTO LAYERS OF BOG ROLL!

Cab Driver:

There once was a lonely cab driver named Frank
whose taxi always seriously stank.
    He'd even tried using *Febreze*
    to put his customers at ease,
but it couldn't mask the smell of his lunchtime wank.

HAEMORRHOIDS

I'VE ONLY GOT ONE THING TO SAY ABOUT HAEMORRHOIDS,
THEY'RE A PAIN IN THE ASS.
AND THAT'S BOTH WHEN I'M GOING TO THE TOILET,
AND PASSING GAS.

AND AS FOR HOW I ENDED UP WITH THEM,
I DON'T HAVE THE FIRST CLUE.
BUT IT'S PROBABLY RELATED TO ALL THE STRAINING,
WHEN I'M SAT ON THE LOO.

AND I INITIALLY PUT UP WITH THE DISCOMFORT,
AND HOPE THEY'LL GO AWAY.
BUT I REALISE A FEW DAYS LATER,
THAT THEY'RE DEFINITELY HERE TO STAY.

SO NOW I HAVE TO TAKE ACTION,
TO PUT AN END TO MY ANAL GRIEF.
AND I RELUCTANTLY HEAD TO THE PHARMACY,
TO SEEK OUT SOME SOOTHING RELIEF.

AND I'M OBVIOUSLY EMBARRASSED TO ASK FOR HELP,
BUT I DON'T HAVE A CHOICE.
SO I STEP UP TO THE COUNTER,
AND EMPLOY MY MOST QUIETEST VOICE.

AND I ASK FOR SOME *PREPARATION H*,
AS I CAN'T SEE IT ON DISPLAY.
AND THE PHARMACIST BOOMS LOUDLY,
"DO YOU WANT THE CREAM OR THE SPRAY?"

WOW! SO MUCH FOR MY PRIVACY, THEN,
AND MY HOPES OF KEEPING MY PROBLEM QUIET.
AND I REGRET NOT STAYING AT HOME,
AND JUST CHANGING MY DIET.

BUT NOW I'M INVESTED,
SO I ASK WHICH REMEDY IS THE BEST.
AS I WANT THE QUICKEST SOLUTION,
TO BE RID OF MY ITCHY, ANAL PEST.

SO THE PHARMACIST PONDERS THIS FOR A MOMENT,
THEN TELLS ME IT'S THE CREAM.
SO I'LL SOON BE FINGERING MY OWN ARSEHOLE,
WHICH WAS HARDLY MY DREAM.

BUT I ACCEPT THE RECOMMENDATION, THOUGH,
AND THEN QUICKLY PAY.
THEN I GRAB MY TUBE OF OINTMENT,
AND SHAMEFULLY SCURRY AWAY!

ATHLETES FOOT

I'VE NEVER BEEN MUCH OF AN ATHLETE,
BUT I'VE HAD ATHLETES FOOT.
AND I SUCCESSFULLY TREATED IT WITH A POWDER,
WHICH LOOKED LIKE WHITE SOOT.

AND IF YOU THOUGHT THAT WAS A TOUGH ONE,
THEN I HATE TO BURST YOUR BUBBLE.
BUT IT'LL TAKE A MUCH HARDER WORD THAN "FOOT",
TO LAND ME IN DEEP RHYMING TROUBLE.

SO LET'S TAKE IT UP A NOTCH, THEN,
AND YOU'RE NOT GONNA BELIEVE THIS.
BUT ATHLETES FOOT'S CLINICAL NAME
IS ACTUALLY *TINEA PEDIS.*

SO HOW'D YOU LIKE THEM APPLES, THEN,
DID YOU LIKE THAT RHYMING BATCH?
AS I JUST RHYMED A WORD,
THAT DIDN'T HAVE AN EXACT MATCH.

SO THAT'S ENOUGH MESSING ABOUT,
AND LET'S GET BACK TO MY FUNGAL INFECTION.
WHICH WAS VERY EASY TO SPOT,
AND DIDN'T TAKE MUCH DETECTION.

AS MY SKIN WAS DRY AND FLAKY,
AND THAT'S THE SKIN BETWEEN MY TOES.
AND THAT'S A SURE SIGN OF ATHLETES FOOT,
WHICH EVERYBODY KNOWS.

AND AS FOR HOW I GOT MY ITCHY RASH,
I'M AFRAID THAT'S BEYOND MY POWER.
BUT IT WAS PROBABLY FROM EXPOSING MYSELF,
IN A CONTAMINATED SHOWER!

Talented Sprinter:

Maria was an extremely talented sprinter
who despised training during the winter.
    She always practised in bare feet,
        as it increased her ability to compete,
and also made it easier to pick up a splinter.

HALITOSIS

TO SAY THAT I'VE GOT BAD BREATH
WOULD BE TO UNDERSTATE THE FACTS.
AS MY BREATH CAN CUT METAL,
AND EASILY MELT WAX.

AND YOU MAY THINK THAT I'M JOKING,
BUT I CAN ASSURE YOU I'M NOT.
AS MY BREATH SMELLS LIKE A BODY,
WHICH IS BEGINNING TO ROT.

AND I'VE HAD THIS CURSE FOR A WHILE,
SINCE ATTENDING SCHOOL IN THE SOUTH.
WHERE I ONCE KNOCKED OUT A TEACHER,
JUST BY OPENING MY MOUTH.

YOU SEE, THE GUY GOT TOO CLOSE,
WHEN HE ASKED ME A QUESTION.
AND I'D WARNED HIM TO KEEP HIS DISTANCE,
THOUGH, IT WAS JUST A SUGGESTION.

AND I'VE TRIED FINDING A RELIABLE CURE, OF COURSE,
BUT THERE'S NOTHING THAT REALLY WORKS.
SO I'LL JUST HAVE TO TREAT MY RAGING HALITOSIS,
AS ONE OF MY MORE UNPLEASANT QUIRKS!

MICROPENIS

I'D LIKE TO SAY THAT I DON'T HAVE ONE OF THESE,
BUT THAT SIMPLY WOULDN'T BE TRUE.
AND IT'S STOPPED ME FROM ATTRACTING A MATE,
AND BEING ABLE TO REGULARLY SCREW.

AND AS FOR THE STUFF AROUND IT,
IT'S ALL OF A RELATIVELY NORMAL SIZE.
AND I'M TALKING ABOUT MY WRINKLY SACK AND BALLS,
WHICH'RE NESTLING BETWEEN MY THIGHS.

AND ACTUALLY HOW SMALL IS SMALL?
IS THE QUESTION THAT'S NOW ON YOUR LIPS.
SO THINK ABOUT TWO LARGE GRAPES AND A LITTLE FINGER,
DANGLING IN FRONT OF MY HIPS.

AND IF THAT ISN'T A GOOD ENOUGH PICTURE,
TO ALLOW YOU TO VISUALISE.
THEN IMAGINE A WOMAN BEING FUCKED BY A STUBBY PENCIL,
AND HER LACK OF ORGASMIC CRIES.

AND I RECKON I COULD EASILY SET A NEW RECORD,
FOR HAVING THE WORLD'S TINIEST DICK.
AND THAT'S ASSUMING THEY COULD EVEN FIND IT,
AND HAD A SMALL ENOUGH MEASURING STICK!

SOGGY BISCUIT

WHEN I HEARD ABOUT THIS UNSAVOURY PRACTICE,
I FIGURED IT COULDN'T BE TRUE.
BUT GOOGLING IT PROVED ME WRONG, HOWEVER,
WHICH IS WHY I'M SHARING IT WITH YOU.

AND THE GAME THAT I HEARD ABOUT,
INVOLVED BLOKES FROM THE BRITISH ARMY.
BUT THEY ALSO PLAY IT IN SOME PUBLIC SCHOOLS,
WHICH IS EVEN MORE BARMY.

SO, SOME GUYS WILL STAND AROUND A BISCUIT,
AND THEN RACE TO HAVE A WANK.
AND I SWEAR THAT THIS IS GENUINE,
AND NOT ME PLAYING A SICK PRANK.

AND THE LAST GUY TO COME ON THE BISCUIT
HAS TO EAT THE WHOLE THING.
AND JUST IMAGINING THAT STICKY SCENARIO
MAKES MY EYES BLOODY STING.

BUT IF I PLAYED THIS MESSY GAME, HOWEVER,
I WOULDN'T HAVE TO WORRY.
BECAUSE, I ALWAYS EJACULATE PREMATURELY
WITHOUT HAVING TO HURRY.

AND THIS IS DEFINITELY THE ONE TIME,
WHEN IT WOULD PAY TO BE QUICK.
SO YOU WOULDN'T HAVE TO EAT THE SOGGY BISCUIT,
AND THEN BE VIOLENTLY SICK!

Soggy Biscuit:

A group of male students from Notre Dame
were playing the soggy biscuit game.
    This race wasn't a sick prank,
    but an actual cookie wank,
where the consuming loser was never the same.

QUEEF

I MENTIONED THIS AT THE END OF *GALS*,
AS PART OF MY RELATIONSHIP ADVICE.
BUT I'M AFRAID THAT COVERING IT ONLY ONCE
JUST WOULDN'T SUFFICE.

SO I'M GOING TO DISCUSS IT IN MORE DETAIL,
AND THIS IS JUST FOR THE GUYS.
SO THEY'LL KNOW WHAT TO DO IF IT OCCURS,
AND WON'T GET TAKEN BY SURPRISE.

NOW, YOU MAY NOT BE AWARE OF THIS WORD,
BUT YOU MIGHT HAVE EXPERIENCED ITS EFFECTS.
AS A QUEEF MOST COMMONLY OCCURS
DURING VIGOROUS SEX.

AND IT'S BASICALLY A VAGINAL FART,
BUT WITHOUT THE SMELL.
AND WOMEN CAN'T SUPRESS IT, EITHER,
WHICH JUST ADDS TO THEIR HELL.

SO THE AIR GETS SUCKED IN AND TRAPPED,
AND THEN IT'S PUSHED BACK OUT.
AND THIS IS WHAT CAUSES
THE UNWANTED EXPLOSIVE BOUT.

AND I'M USING THE WORD "EXPLOSIVE",
AS A QUEEF CAN BE VERY LOUD.
WHICH LEAVES THE WOMAN WHO DEALT IT
FEELING ANYTHING BUT PROUD.

SO, IF YOUR GIRL DOES QUEEF DURING SEX,
THEN DON'T FREAK OUT OR DUCK FOR COVER.
JUST CONTINUE LIKE NOTHING HAPPENED, DUDE,
LIKE AN EXPERIENCED LOVER.

AND YOUR GAL WILL BE HORRIFIED THAT HER VAGINA
CAN MAKE SUCH A DISTURBING NOISE.
AND SHE'D APPRECIATE YOUR DISCRETION, DUDE,
AND YOU NOT SHARING IT WITH THE BOYS!

Sunny Tenerife:

Giselle lived and worked exclusively in sunny Tenerife
and was both a prosperous and competent thief.
Then she got caught stealing a painting,
but not due to stupidity or fainting,
but because she unexpectedly emitted a queef.

41

WOT! NO BOG ROLL

THIS TOPIC HAS THE POTENTIAL TO BE REALLY AMUSING,
SO I'M GOING TO TAKE MY SWEET TIME.
BECAUSE I STILL HAVEN'T MANAGED, YET,
TO WRITE THAT ONE TRULY HYSTERICAL RHYME.

AND I HATE FINDING THERE'S NO BOG ROLL LEFT,
WHEN I'M DESPERATE TO TAKE A DUMP.
AS I'M USUALLY SITTING ON AN ELEPHANT,
OR HAVE A TURTLE'S HEAD POKING OUT OF MY RUMP.

AND AS MUCH AS I HATE FINDING NO TOILET PAPER,
I DETEST RUNNING OUT EVEN MORE.
AS I'LL HARDLY BE IN A POSITION AT THAT POINT
TO NIP TO THE LOCAL FUCKING STORE.

BUT IT'S NOT RUNNING OUT THAT REALLY ANGERS ME
IT'S THAT I DIDN'T CHECK FIRST.
AND AS MAKING STUPID MISTAKES ACTUALLY GO,
IT'S GOTTA BE ONE OF THE WORST.

AND IF YOU HAPPEN TO GET INTO THIS SITUATION,
STUCK BETWEEN THE HARD PLACE AND THE ROCK.
THEN DO NOT FUCKING PANIC, MY FRIEND,
AS YOU CAN ALWAYS SACRIFICE A SOCK.

AND YOU WON'T BE THE FIRST TO DO THIS, OF COURSE,
SO DON'T WORRY OR DESPAIR.
AS THROWING AWAY A SHITTY SOCK OR TWO
IS HARDLY WORTH PULLING OUT YOUR HAIR.

AND EVEN IF YOU FIND PLENTY OF LOO ROLL AT WORK,
IT COULD STILL BE THE REALLY CHEAP STUFF.
WHICH IS MORE LIKE WIPING WITH BLOODY SANDPAPER,
AND EXTREMELY ANALLY ROUGH.

AND THEY BUY THE REALLY CHEAP CRAP, OF COURSE,
SO PEOPLE WON'T TAKE IT HOME.
AS NO ONE'S GONNA STEAL TOILET TISSUE
THAT CAN TAKE THE SHINE OFF OF CHROME!

DIRTY SUGAR

THIS IS NEVER AN ISSUE IN MY OWN HOUSE,
BECAUSE I HAPPILY LIVE ON MY OWN.
SO IT'S NOT UNTIL I ACTUALLY GO INTO WORK,
THAT I ENTER THE DIRTY SUGAR ZONE.

AND I JUST WANT TO START MY WORKING DAY,
WITH A LOVELY, FRESH MUG OF COFFEE.
BUT I HAVE TO DEAL WITH THE RANCID SUGAR,
THAT'S TAKEN ON THE COLOUR AND TEXTURE OF TOFFEE.

AND THIS IS THE PROBLEM WITH A KITCHEN,
THAT A HUNDRED PEOPLE SHARE.
AS YOU GET UNHYGIENIC WANKERS,
WHO JUST DON'T FUCKING CARE.

AND THEY'RE HAPPY TO DUMP ALL SORTS OF SHIT
INTO THE SHARED SUGAR BOWL.
UNTIL IT LOOKS LESS LIKE SNOWY SUGAR,
AND MORE LIKE LUMPS OF BLOODY COAL.

AND SEEING SUGAR CONTAMINATED WITH BITS OF CEREAL
IS DISGUSTINGLY OBSCENE.
SO I DON'T THINK I'M ASKING FOR TOO MUCH,
TO KEEP THE FUCKING SUGAR CLEAN.

BUT I KNOW THAT MOST OF THE ANIMALS I WORK WITH
WON'T BE ABLE TO COMPLY.
WHICH IS WHY IN THE BOTTOM DRAWER OF MY DESK,
I'VE NOW GOT A SECRET SUGAR SUPPLY!

Men's Loo:

There once was a delicate office worker named Stu
who never relished visiting the men's loo.
 He'd often find something floating and nasty,
  which ruined his lunchtime pasty,
in the form of some other bloke's poo.

COMPLAINING

WE COMPLAIN ABOUT THIS,
AND WE COMPLAIN ABOUT THAT.
WHEN PEOPLE ARE TOO THIN,
OR IF THEY'RE TOO FAT.

AND WE COMPLAIN ABOUT EVERYTHING, REALLY,
WHICH SHOULD COME AS NO SURPRISE.
AND YOU KNOW THAT I'M RIGHT,
AND NOT TELLING YOU LIES.

AND WE COMPLAIN ABOUT OUR FAMILIES,
AND ALSO OUR FRIENDS.
AND THESE ARE TWO SUBJECTS,
WHERE THE COMPLAINING NEVER ENDS.

AND WE COULD EVEN COMPLAIN FOR THE OLYMPICS,
IF WE WERE GIVEN HALF A CHANCE.
THOUGH, I'M NOT SURE HOW WE'D DO,
AGAINST THE STIFF COMPETITION FROM FRANCE.

AND WE COMPLAIN ABOUT WHAT WE EAT,
AND THEN WHAT WE DRINK.
AND THE STATE OF OUR KITCHENS,
ESPECIALLY THE SINK.

AND WE COMPLAIN ABOUT WORK,
AND WHO WE HATE THE MOST.
AND WE DO THIS INCESSANTLY,
EVEN DURING BREAKFAST OVER TOAST.

AND WE COMPLAIN ABOUT QUEUEING,
AND THE POOR SERVICE AT THE BANK.
AND THEN ABOUT HOW MUCH IT COSTS,
TO REFILL OUR CAR'S FUEL TANK.

AND WE COMPLAIN ABOUT THE SCREAMING KIDS
RUNNING WILD IN THE SUPERMARKET.
AND ABOUT THAT FLASHY IDIOT IN THE *PORSCHE,*
WHO OBVIOUSLY CAN'T REVERSE PARK IT.

AND WE COMPLAIN ABOUT OUR NEIGHBOURS,
AND HOW MUCH NOISE THEY MAKE.
AND WE EVEN COMPLAIN ABOUT NOT KNOWING
HOW MUCH MORE WE CAN TAKE.

AND WE COMPLAIN ABOUT OUR SLOW BROADBAND,
WHEN IT AFFECTS OUR ONLINE GAMING.
AND WE EVEN COMPLAIN ABOUT THE PEOPLE,
WHO ARE ALWAYS BLOODY COMPLAINING!

SEX

WHEN IT COMES TO HAVING SEX,
MEN TURN ON QUICKLY, JUST LIKE A LIGHT.
BUT IT TAKES A GREAT DEAL LONGER
FOR A WOMAN TO FEEL READY AND RIGHT.

AND WOMEN HAVE ALL THE SEXUAL KNOWHOW,
WHEREAS MEN ARE NAÏVELY DUMB.
SOME OF THEM EVEN RECITE THE ALPHABET BACKWARDS,
HOPING NOT TO PREMATURELY COME.

AND WOMEN NEED TO FEEL A CONNECTION,
AND BUILD UP SOME TRUST.
WHEREAS, MEN ARE ALWAYS READY TO GO
ON MAXIMUM THRUST.

AND YOU'D BETTER MAKE A SERIOUS EFFORT, GUYS,
TO FIND HER G-SPOT.
OTHERWISE YOUR PARTNER WON'T REACH ORGASM,
OR EVEN GET VERY HOT.

SO, START WITH SOME FOREPLAY,
INCLUDING PLENTY OF TOUCHING AND KISSING.
AND DON'T BE AFRAID TO ASK FOR ADVICE,
ABOUT THE THINGS THAT YOU'RE MISSING.

AND PRETTY SOON YOU'LL BE FULLY AROUSED,
AND READY TO PENETRATE YOUR MATE.
BUT DO TRY TO LAST MORE THAN A MINUTE,
BEFORE YOU EJACULATE.

AND WHAT ABOUT FANTASY COSTUMES,
WITH STOCKINGS OR RUBBER AND LATEX.
NOT THAT MOST GUYS NEED THE HELP OF UNIFORMS
TO GET THEM READY FOR SEX.

AND IF YOU'RE NOT IN TO ROLEPLAYING, LADIES,
AND WEARING THOSE SEXY OUTFITS.
THEN AT LEAST LET YOUR GUY OCCASIONALLY MASTURBATE
WITH THE AID OF YOUR TITS.

AND SEX IS NOW NO LONGER
JUST PURELY ABOUT COMBINATIONS OF GIRLS AND BOYS.
AS YOU'VE GOT TO TAKE INTO ACCOUNT
YOUR PARTNER'S DRAWER FULL OF SEX TOYS.

AND MORE AND MORE WOMEN NOW
ARE USING A MAGICAL TOY CALLED A *RABBIT*.
WHICH IS FAR MORE RELIABLE THAN A MAN,
AND COULD EASILY BECOME A PERMANENT HABIT!

PHONING IN SICK

NOW, I KNOW THIS IS WRONG,
AND IT'S GONNA MAKE ME SEEM LIKE A DICK.
BUT I STILL GET A NOTICEABLE RUSH
FROM PHONING IN SICK.

AND I DON'T MEAN THE OCCASIONS, OF COURSE,
WHEN I'M GENUINELY ILL.
AS IT'S THE INSTANCES WHEN I PLAY HOOKY
THAT GIVE ME A SERIOUS THRILL.

AND THIS IS WHAT'S KNOWN IN THE TRADE,
AS A VERY GUILTY PLEASURE.
WHICH I ONLY DO OCCASIONALLY,
WHEN I'M IN NEED OF SOME LEISURE.

AND I MAY JUST NEED SOME EXTRA DOWNTIME,
TO GET THINGS STRAIGHT IN MY HEAD.
UNLESS I'M HAVING ONE OF THOSE DAYS,
WHEN I CAN'T BE ARSED TO GET OUT OF BED!

ELDERLY COUPLES

SEEING AN ELDERLY COUPLE HOLDING HANDS,
AS THEY WALK DOWN THE STREET.
REALLY WARMS MY LONELY HEART,
AND EVOKES EMOTIONS THAT ARE SWEET.

AND I KNOW THEY'VE PROBABLY BEEN TOGETHER,
FOR FORTY OR FIFTY-PLUS YEARS.
WHICH PROVES THAT TRUE LOVE IS ETERNAL,
AND WORTH ALL THE BLOOD, SWEAT AND TEARS.

AND IT ALSO DEMONSTRATES WHAT'S POSSIBLE,
IF YOU FIND THE PERFECT ONE.
AS LIFE BECOMES MUCH MORE MANAGEABLE,
AND A HELLUVA LOT MORE FUN.

AND THEY'VE SAVOURED ALL THE GREAT TIMES,
AND SURVIVED THE TERRIBLE LOWS.
AS WELL AS ENJOYING ALL THEIR BLESSINGS,
AND SHARING ALL THEIR WOES.

AND THEY'VE FOUND THEIR LOVING SOULMATE,
AND THEY'VE BEATEN ALL THE ODDS.
AND I TRULY HOPE THEY'RE STILL HOLDING HANDS,
WHEN THEY GO TO MEET THEIR GODS!

SWEARING

HAVING A GOOD SWEARY-SWEARY SWEAR-SWEAR
ALWAYS BRIGHTENS MY MOOD.
BUT DON'T WORRY IF YOU HATE EXPLETIVES,
AS THIS RHYME'S NOT GONNA BE RUDE.

AND AS MUCH AS I LOVE CURSING,
HEARING SOMEONE ELSE SWEAR IS BETTER.
ESPECIALLY WHEN THEY'RE INVENTIVE,
AND A BIT OF A PROFANITY TRENDSETTER.

AND THE STANDARD CURSE WORDS ARE OK,
WHEN YOU NEED TO QUICKLY SETTLE A SCORE.
BUT I MUCH PREFER HEARING OBSCENE WORDS,
WHICH I'VE NEVER ACTUALLY HEARD BEFORE.

AND I RECENTLY WATCHED THE FILM *DEADPOOL*,
WHICH HAD AN IMPRESSIVE SWEARING TALLY.
BUT JUST IN TERMS OF SHEER INVENTIVENESS,
YOU CAN'T BEAT THE GUYS FROM *SILICON VALLEY*.

AND SWEAR WORDS DON'T HAVE TO BE THAT OFFENSIVE,
IN ORDER TO BE FUN.
THOUGH, COCK-JUGGLING-THUNDER-CUNT
IS STILL MY MOST FAVOURITE ONE.

AND, YEAH, I KNOW, I KNOW,
I SAID THIS RHYME WASN'T GONNA BE RUDE.
BUT I'M AFRAID THAT'S WHAT YOU GET
FOR TRUSTING SUCH A CHILDISH DUDE!

Misdemeanour:

There once was a wild teenager named Geena

who was arrested on a misdemeanour.

    She was drunk in the street

    with no shoes on her feet

and her language couldn't have been fucking obscener.

#PIGGATE

I SHOULD PROBABLY START BY USING THE WORD "ALLEGEDLY",
SO THAT I DON'T GET SUED.
BUT I SERIOUSLY DOUBT THAT DAVID CAMERON
READS STUFF THAT'S THIS CHEAP OR CRUDE.

AND NOW WE'VE GOT THAT OUT OF THE WAY,
WE CAN GET TO THE REAL MEAT OF THE MATTER.
WHICH HAD THE INTERNET AWASH,
WITH ALL SORTS OF PIG-BASED CHATTER.

NOW, THIS UNOFFICIAL BIOGRAPHY WAS WRITTEN,
ALL ABOUT DAVID CAMERON'S LIFE.
WHICH STATED ALL SORTS OF CRAZY SHIT,
AND DELIBERATELY CUT DEEP LIKE A KNIFE.

AND IT ALLEGES THAT CAMERON STUCK HIS DICK,
IN THE MOUTH OF A DEAD PIG.
AND AS NEWS STORIES WENT IN 2015,
THIS ONE WAS SENSATIONALLY BIG.

SO, THIS UNCORROBORATED ANECDOTE
WAS ATTRIBUTED TO AN ANONYMOUS MP.
AND IT WAS SUPPOSED TO BE BACKED BY A PHOTOGRAPH,
WHICH WE NEVER GOT TO SEE.

AND CAMERON DIDN'T DIGNIFY THE ALLEGATION WITH A REPLY,
AND HE DIDN'T HIT THE ROOF.
BUT THEN, WHY THE HELL WOULD HE,
WHEN THERE WASN'T ANY CREDIBLE PROOF.

AND THIS EVENT SUPPOSEDLY TOOK PLACE,
AS PART OF A UNIVERSITY HAZING.
BUT SOME JOURNALISTS LOOKED INTO IT,
AND DIDN'T FIND ANYTHING AMAZING.

AND THEY FIGURED IT WAS ALL BULLSHIT,
AND JUST SOMEONE BEING MALICIOUS.
AND GIVEN THE COMPLETE LACK OF EVIDENCE,
THEY'D BE RIGHT TO BE SUSPICIOUS.

SO, THE STORY WAS THEN LINKED TO *BLACK MIRROR*,
WHICH WAS CHARLIE BROOKER'S TV SHOW.
BUT HE DENIED ANY PRIOR KNOWLEDGE OF THE ACT,
AND SAID HE HONESTLY DIDN'T KNOW.

AND I KNOW IT SEEMS LIKE THE SORT OF THING,
WHICH MIGHT HAPPEN AT A PRIVATE SCHOOL.
BUT I DOUBT THAT IT ACTUALLY OCCURRED, THOUGH,
AS CAMERON'S JUST NOT THAT INTERESTING OR COOL!

#EDSTONE

I HAD TO CHECK THAT I WASN'T DREAMING,
WHEN THIS BIZARRE STORY FIRST BROKE.
AND EVEN THOUGH I WAS DEFINITELY WIDE AWAKE,
I STILL FIGURED IT WAS A JOKE.

BUT THE JOKE WAS ON THE LABOUR PARTY, THOUGH,
WHO SUFFERED A HUMILIATING ELECTION DEFEAT.
WHICH IS EXACTLY WHAT THEY BLOODY DESERVED
FOR WASTING 30-GRAND ON A USELESS LUMP OF CONCRETE.

NOW, THE PLEDGE STONE WAS UNVEILED IN HASTINGS,
WHERE IT HAD BEEN SECRETLY ERECTED.
AND WAS CARVED WITH SIX KEY PLEDGES
THAT WOULDN'T BE LOST AFTER LABOUR WAS ELECTED.

BUT THE STUNT WAS A COMPLETE DISASTER, THOUGH,
AND QUICKLY RIDICULED ON SOCIAL MEDIA.
AND THE STONE BECAME SUCH MONUMENTAL NEWS,
THAT IT GOT ITS OWN PAGE ON *WIKIPEDIA.*

AND THE STONE WAS CARVED WITH ED MILIBAND'S SIGNATURE,
WHICH HE THOUGHT WAS A GREAT IDEA.
BUT HE WAS JUST SIGNING HIS OWN DEATH WARRANT,
AND PUTTING AN END TO HIS POLITICAL CAREER.

AND HE WAS QUICKLY REPLACED AS PARTY LEADER,
WHICH WASN'T A BIG SURPRISE.
AND THEN THE STONE DISAPPEARED ABRUPTLY,
AMIDST A SHROUD OF DENIALS AND LIES.

AND THE STONE EASILY WEIGHED TWO TONNES,
AND WAS WELL OVER EIGHT FEET TALL.
AND IT SIMPLY VANISHED INTO THIN AIR,
AFTER LABOUR HAD PACKED UP THEIR STALL.

AND NO ONE KNOWS WHO BUILT THE STONE, EITHER,
AND SUSPECT IT CAME FROM OVERSEAS.
BUT LABOUR'S STILL STAYING TIGHT-LIPPED ON THE SUBJECT,
IN SPITE OF ALL THE MEDIAS' PLEAS.

AND MOST PEOPLE BELIEVE THE STONE WAS DESTROYED,
BUT I SAW IT FOR SALE ON *EBAY*.
BUT THEY WANTED NEARLY TWO-GRAND FOR IT, THOUGH,
WHICH I THOUGHT WAS TOO MUCH TO PAY!

BAD ADVERTS

I'VE ALREADY MOANED A LITTLE ABOUT BAD ADVERTS
IN A PREVIOUS BOOK.
BUT IT'S TIME TO STOP PULLING MY PUNCHES,
AND DELIVER A SERIOUS RIGHT HOOK.

AND THERE ARE A MULTITUDE OF TERRIBLE ADVERTS,
CURRENTLY BEING SHOWN ON TV.
BUT I'LL JUST GRIPE ABOUT MY WORST ONES,
TO SEE IF YOU AGREE.

SO, I'M GONNA START WITH THE *VANISH* ADVERT,
WHICH FILLS ME WITH PATHOLOGICAL RAGE.
AND EVEN THINKING ABOUT IT NOW,
MAKES ME WANT TO SET FIRE TO THIS PAGE.

AND THEIR TEDIOUS MESSAGE IS ALWAYS THE SAME,
IN THAT WE ONLY NEED ONE SCOOP.
AND THAT'S FOR DEALING WITH ANY TYPE OF STAIN,
FROM RED WINE TO BABY POOP.

AND THEY ALSO WANT US TO LIKE THEM ON *FACEBOOK*,
AND FOLLOW THEM ON *TWITTER*.
BUT I JUST WANT TO FIND THE PERSON RESPONSIBLE,
AND STUFF THEIR HEAD IN THE SHITTER.

AND I KNOW IT'S JUST A HARMLESS PROMOTIONAL TOOL,
AND SHOULDN'T FILL ME WITH SUCH HATE.
BUT I CAN'T STOP IT FROM PUSHING MY BUTTONS,
AND MAKING ME UNCONTROLLABLY IRATE.

SO, THAT'S ENOUGH VENTING ABOUT *VANISH*, THEN,
AND NOW LET'S MOVE ON TO *LYNX*.
WHERE THE AD MAKERS ARE STILL USING SEX TO SELL,
WHICH I THINK SERIOUSLY STINKS.

AND THEIR SPECTACULAR LACK OF VISION
LEAVES ME FEELING VERY DEPRESSED AND SICK.
AS NO AMOUNT OF FUCKING BODY SPRAY,
IS GONNA MAKE A WOMAN SUCK MY DICK.

SO, I'M GOING TO FINISH WITH A LENGTHY BANK ADVERT,
WHICH I FIND PARTICULARLY ANNOYING.
AS IT'S JUST FURTHER PROOF THAT THE AD PEOPLE
CAN'T PRODUCE ANYTHING WORTH ENJOYING.

AND IT'S THE ONE WITH THE GUY ON A BUS
WHO LOSES HIS RAGGEDY OLD SCARF.
AND DESPITE ITS RETURN BY SOMEONE FROM THE BANK,
IT DOESN'T CAUSE ME TO LAUGH.

AND MY LIFE WON'T SUDDENLY BE MADE BETTER,
JUST BY JOINING A SPECIFIC BANK.
WHICH IS WHY I THINK THE WHOLE PREMISE FOR THE AD,
IS A COMPLETE LOAD OF DOG-WANK!

WOMB TRANSPLANT

I'VE JUST SEEN AN INTERESTING ARTICLE ON THE WEB,
ABOUT SUCCESSFULLY TRANSPLANTING A WOMB.
AND I WONDER IF THE REASON WHY THEY DID IT
WAS BECAUSE THE BABY NEEDED MORE ROOM.

BUT ALL JOKING ASIDE FOR A MOMENT,
I THINK THIS IS SCIENCE PROGRESSING AT ITS ABSOLUTE BEST.
AS LONG AS THEY DON'T START RELOCATING THEM INTO MEN,
WHICH WOULD BE SERIOUSLY HARD TO DIGEST!

Reporter:

Ken the reporter always left it late to go jogging,
after he'd finished work and his online blogging.
    He needed it to be dark
    so he could run to the park
and join the other voyeurs taking part in some dogging.

TOMATO SKIN

I DON'T HATE TOMATOES PER SE,
JUST THEIR INDESTRUCTIBLE SKIN.
AND NO MATTER HOW LONG I CHEW IT FOR,
I JUST CAN'T SEEM TO WIN.

AND I'LL GRIND AWAY AT IT FOR BLOODY AGES,
AND THEN TO MY UTTER DISBELIEF.
SOME HOURS AFTER I'VE FINISHED EATING,
I'LL FIND SOME TOMATO SKIN IN MY TEETH.

SO THEY SHOULD USE IT TO COVER SPACE SHUTTLES,
OR TO TARMAC THE ROADS.
AS TOMATO SKIN IS ONE STUBBORN SUBSTANCE,
WHICH NEVER ACTUALLY ERODES.

AND YOU'RE PROBABLY THINKING I SHOULD JUST AVOID IT,
WHICH IS HARDLY A SCOOP.
BUT THAT'S NOT SO EASY TO DO, MY FRIEND,
WHEN YOU LOVE EATING VEGETABLE SOUP!

FLATULENCE

I THINK THIS ISSUE IS MEDICAL,
ALTHOUGH I'M NOT ABSOLUTELY SURE.
BUT AFTER FORTY YEARS OF UNHEALTHY FARTING,
I DEFINITELY KNOW THERE'S NO CURE.

AND I'VE TRIED CHANGING MY DIET,
AND WATCHING WHAT I EAT.
BUT I'M STILL PASSING UNBREATHABLE GAS
FROM THE HOLE IN MY SEAT.

AND I KNOW WHAT YOU'RE THINKING.
HOW BAD CAN MY FARTS ACTUALLY BE?
BUT HAVE YOU EVER SMELT A FLOATER,
THAT'S JUST BEEN PULLED FROM THE SEA.

AND PERHAPS THAT'S THE PROBLEM.
MAYBE MY GUTS ARE SLOWLY ROTTING AWAY.
WHICH WOULD CERTAINLY HELP TO EXPLAIN THINGS,
AT THE END OF THE DAY.

AND I'M NOT JOKING ABOUT THE SMELL,
AS IT'S REALLY QUITE FOUL.
AND IT CAN BE DESCRIBED BY MANY OTHER WORDS,
THAT DON'T START WITH A VOWEL.

PHEW! THAT WAS A CLOSE ONE,
AS I NEARLY CAME UNSTUCK.
BUT I'M SURE THERE'LL COME A TIME,
WHEN I RUN OUT OF RHYMING LUCK.

BUT THAT TIME ISN'T NOW, THOUGH,
SO LET'S MOVE THINGS ALONG.
AS I'VE GOT TO FIND THE RIGHT WORD,
TO DESCRIBE MY TERRIBLE PONG.

AND I COULD MENTION BOILING CABBAGE,
OR BURNING MUSHY PEAS.
BUT THESE SMELLS DON'T EVEN COME CLOSE,
AND NOR DOES STINKY BLUE CHEESE.

SO, WHAT ABOUT SMELLING DECAYING GARBAGE, THEN,
OR SNIFFING A SEWER?
BUT COMPARED TO MY FOUL FARTS,
THEY'RE BOTH FAIRLY FRAGRANTLY PURE.

SO, WE NEED TO GO MUCH MORE EXTREME, THEN,
LIKE SMELLING A DEAD RAT.
OR CATCHING A WHIFF FROM THE CARCASS,
OF A MAGGOT-INFESTED CAT!

CONSTIPATION

I'VE GOT NO REAL IDEA WHY,
BUT I CAN'T TAKE A CRAP.
AND IT'S STARTING TO PLAY HAVOC
WITH MY INTESTINAL MAP.

AND I'M STILL SHOVELLING THE SAME FOOD
INTO MY BOTTOMLESS PIT.
SO I JUST DON'T UNDERSTAND
WHY I CAN'T SQUEEZE OUT A SHIT.

SO EVERY TIME I FEEL A RUMBLE,
I DASH TO THE LOO.
WHERE I PATIENTLY SIT,
HOPING TO POO.

BUT ABSOLUTELY NOTHING HAPPENS,
NO MATTER HOW MUCH I STRAIN.
AND I EVENTUALLY THROW IN THE TOWEL,
AS I CAN'T TAKE THE PAIN.

SO THIS CONTINUES FOR ANOTHER DAY,
WITH NO SIGN OF A STOOL.
THEN I CONSIDER PURCHASING A REMEDY,
EVEN THOUGH I'LL FEEL LIKE A FOOL.

AND I HAVE TO DO SOMETHING SOON,
BEFORE I'M SHITTING A CONCRETE LOG.
AS I DON'T WANT TO HAVE AN ANEURYSM,
WHILE I'M SQUATTING ON THE BOG.

SO I SWALLOW AN HERBAL REMEDY,
AND THEN WAIT FOR IT TO KICK IN.
THINKING, THIS IS A HIGH PRICE TO PAY
FOR MY DIETARY SIN.

BUT IT STILL TAKES BLOODY AGES,
BEFORE I FINALLY GET MY RELIEF.
SO I DECIDE TO CHANGE MY DIET,
TO AVOID ANY MORE TOILET-BASED GRIEF.

AND I HOPE YOU'VE LEARNED A LESSON, TOO,
FROM MY TALE OF CONSTIPATED WOE.
WHICH IS, TO PUT SOME DECENT FIBRE IN YOUR DIET,
BEFORE YOU FIND YOU CAN'T GO!

CRABS

I WANTED TO COVER STIs IN GENERAL,
BUT WORRIED I MIGHT BE CROSSING A LINE.
AND THEN I JUST THOUGHT, *"FUCK IT!"*,
AND DECIDED THAT BENDING IT A LITTLE WOULD BE FINE.

AND THE WHOLE POINT OF THESE RHYMES, OF COURSE,
IS TO TRY AND MAKE YOU LAUGH.
SO HERE'S HOW I CONTRACTED CRABS
AT THE BASE OF MY STAFF.

NOW, I GOT THEM FROM A BLONDE CALLED LISA,
WHO WAS A BIT OF A SLUT.
BUT I WAS VERY YOUNG AT THE TIME,
AND JUST DESPERATE TO RUT.

AND RUTTING IS AN ANIMAL TERM,
USED FOR A PERIOD OF SHAGGING.
WHICH I CHECKED IN A DICTIONARY,
TO ENSURE MY VOCABULARY ISN'T FLAGGING.

SO I'M SURE YOU KNOW WHAT CRABS ARE,
WITHOUT ME HAVING TO EXPLAIN.
AND ALTHOUGH THEY FEED ON BLOOD,
THEY CREATE MORE ITCHINESS THAN PAIN.

AND THEY LIVE IN OUR PUBES,
AND OTHER COARSE HAIR.
WHICH IS WHY I NOW SHAVE MY PUBIC REGION,
WITH SOME CONSIDERABLE CARE.

BUT THEY CAN ALSO LIVE IN THE LASHES, THOUGH,
AROUND OUR EYES.
AND ME LEARNING THAT UNSAVOURY FACT
CAME AS A MAJOR SURPRISE.

BUT NOW THAT I KNOW IT, OF COURSE,
I CAN HAPPILY SHARE IT WITH YOU.
SO YOU'LL BE MUCH BETTER PREPARED,
WHEN CHOOSING YOUR NEXT PARTNER TO SCREW!

HAND DRYERS

WHEN IT COMES TO PUBLIC HAND DRYERS,
I'M ANYTHING BUT SMITTEN.
IT'S LIKE MY HANDS ARE BEING BLOWN ON,
BY AN ASTHMATIC KITTEN.

AND THAT'S ASSUMING THEY EVEN WORK, OF COURSE,
WHICH MOST OF THEM DO NOT.
SO I'LL BE FORCED TO USE MY TROUSERS INSTEAD,
WHICH LEAVES A WET SPOT.

AND NOW IT LOOKS TO THE ENTIRE WORLD,
LIKE I'VE JUST PISSED MY PANTS.
WHICH MY MATES ARE HAPPY TO POINT OUT,
BECAUSE THEY'RE ALL INFANTS.

AND I KNOW, TECHNICALLY, THAT DOESN'T RHYME,
BUT I'M DOING MY BEST.
SO STOP BUSTING MY BALLS FOR CHRIST'S SAKE,
AND JUST READ THE REST.

AND WHY IS A DECENT HAND DRYER,
SO FUCKING DIFFICULT TO PRODUCE?
ONE THAT BLOWS PROPER HOT AIR,
AND HAS SOME SERIOUS JUICE.

AND EVEN THE SNAZZY *DYSON* ONES,
WHICH YOU PUT YOUR HANDS INSIDE.
ARE JUST AS CRAP AS THE BLOWERS,
AND DON'T STEM THE WET TIDE.

BUT MY BIGGEST PROBLEM WITH HAND DRYERS
IS THAT THEY DON'T GET RID OF THE BUGS.
THEY JUST LEAVE THEM ON OUR WET HANDS,
AND MAKE US ALL LOOK LIKE MUGS.

AND THAT'S WHY I HONESTLY THINK IT'S TIME,
TO BRING BACK THE HUMBLE PAPER TOWEL.
AS, NOT ONLY WILL THEY DRY OUR HANDS PROPERLY,
BUT THEY'LL MAKE MY TEMPER LESS FOUL!

SKY REMOTE

THIS IS SOMETHING ELSE THAT WINDS ME UP,
AND IS THEREFORE ANOTHER PET HATE.
AND IF YOU HAPPEN TO SUBSCRIBE TO *SKY*,
THEN I'M SURE YOU CAN RELATE.

AND IT HAS TO DO WITH THE DISPLAYED WARNING,
WHEN THE REMOTE'S BATTERIES ARE RUNNING LOW.
WHICH SERIOUSLY PISSES ME OFF
AS THERE'S JUST NO WAY THEY CAN KNOW.

SO, WHEN THE ANNOYING MESSAGE POPS UP,
I HAPPILY GIVE IT THE FINGER.
BUT THIS DOESN'T SOLVE THE PROBLEM, THOUGH,
AND THE WARNING CONTINUES TO LINGER.

SO THEN I TAKE THE BATTERIES OUT,
AND QUICKLY SWAP THEM AROUND.
WHICH FOOLS THE SYSTEM INTO THINKING,
THAT SOME NEW BATTERIES HAVE BEEN FOUND.

AND THIS GETS RID OF THE STUPID WARNING,
FOR ABOUT THREE MONTHS OR SO.
BUT THEN IT COMES BACK WITH A VENGEANCE,
AND CAUSES MY ANGER TO GROW.

SO NOW I HAVE TO FIDDLE WITH THE BATTERIES AGAIN,
TO MAKE IT GO AWAY.
BECAUSE THE WARNING MESSAGE IS JUST BULLSHIT
AND I'M NOT GOING TO PAY.

AND THIS CONTINUES ON A LOOP,
AND DRIVES ME CLOSE TO SHEDDING TEARS.
BECAUSE I ONLY USE QUALITY BATTERIES,
WHICH LAST FOR FUCKING YEARS.

AND I KNOW IT'S A BLOODY SCAM.
AND I KNOW THERE'S NO WAY THEY CAN TELL.
SO I FIGURE *SKY* ARE ONLY DOING IT,
BECAUSE THEY OWN SHARES IN *DURACELL!*

PLASTIC PACKAGING

I SERIOUSLY ABHOR ALL THE PLASTIC PACKAGING,
WHICH HAS BEEN VACUUM-SEALED.
THE STUFF YOU HAVE TO ATTACK WITH A MACHETE,
BECAUSE IT CAN'T BE HUMANLY PEELED.

AND I HAVE TO TOTALLY DESTROY THE PACKAGE,
JUST TO GET AT WHAT'S INSIDE.
AND WITH NO SMALL AMOUNT OF RISK,
TO MY OWN PERSONAL HIDE.

AND YOU MAY THINK I'M KIDDING ABOUT THE DANGER,
BUT I CAN ASSURE YOU I'M NOT.
AS I COULD EASILY SLICE OPEN A FINGER,
AND THEN BLEED QUITE A LOT.

AND I'VE ONLY PURCHASED A POXY CABLE,
OR A LITTLE USB STICK.
NOT SOME FORM OF NUCLEAR MATERIAL,
WHOSE CASING NEEDS TO BE IMPREGNABLY THICK.

SO I THINK THE MANUFACTURERS DO THIS DELIBERATELY,
JUST TO MAKE US IRATE.
WHILE THEY HAPPILY PAD THEIR FAT WALLETS,
AND CHANGE THE PLANET'S ECOLOGICAL STATE.

AND I'D LOVE TO MEET THE ORIGINAL INVENTOR, THOUGH,
AND PUNCH HIM IN THE FACE.
FOR INVENTING THE MOST ANNOYING THING I'VE FOUND,
IN THE ENTIRE HUMAN RACE!

Plastic Cock-ring:

Norman was a naive husband from Tring
whose wife gave him a plastic cock-ring.
It was supposed to help him last longer
and make his orgasm stronger,
but its mis-fitment just made his eyes sting.

NAD CRUSH

THIS RHYME IS STRICTLY FOR THE GUYS,
SO ANY GALS SHOULD MOVE ALONG.
BECAUSE YOU'RE NOT GOING TO GET THIS,
UNLESS YOU'RE PACKING A SCHLONG.

AND WE HAVE TO DEAL WITH ALL SORTS OF PAIN,
DO US POOR, HENPECKED LADS.
BUT NOTHING ACTUALLY HURTS US MORE,
THAN WHEN WE SIT ON OUR OWN NADS.

AND ACCIDENTALLY CRUSHING OUR OWN BALLS
IS A LOT EASIER THAN YOU'D THINK.
AND EVEN THOUGH WE DON'T CRY OUT,
IT STILL MAKES US SERIOUSLY BLINK.

AND WE'RE BLINKING AWAY OUR SILENT TEARS,
WHILE WE DEAL WITH THE SHOCK.
THEN WE HAVE TO SHOVE OUR HAND DOWN OUR PANTS,
TO REPOSITION OUR COCK!

KIDS

I'M TALKING ABOUT THE KIDS IN THE SUPERMARKET,
THE ONES RUNNING RIOT.
THE ONES I'D LIKE TO STRANGLE,
JUST TO GET SOME PEACE AND QUIET.

AND I KNOW THIS IS CONTROVERSIAL,
AND I SHOULD PROBABLY KEEP IT TO MYSELF.
BUT I'D LIKE TO BE ABLE TO CONCENTRATE,
WHEN I'M GRABBING MY GROCERIES OFF THE SHELF.

AND I'M SURE THERE ARE MANY OTHERS OUT THERE,
WHO ARE ANNOYED BY THIS AS WELL.
WHO HATE IT AS MUCH AS I DO,
WHEN THE STORE BECOMES A JUVENILE SCREAMING HELL.

BUT THEY JUST SHAKE THEIR HEADS, THOUGH,
AND GO QUIETLY ON THEIR WAY.
AS THEY DON'T WANT TO MAKE A SCENE,
OR THEY DON'T KNOW WHAT TO SAY.

BUT I GET IN THE OFFENDING PARENTS' FACES, HOWEVER,
AND THEN I LOUDLY BARK.
GET YOUR LITTLE MONSTERS UNDER CONTROL,
BECAUSE WE'RE NOT IN THE FUCKING PARK!

DRINKING

IT'S THE END OF THE WEEK,
AND I'VE JUST BEEN PAID.
SO IT'S TIME TO GET MY DRINK ON,
FOLLOWED BY TRYING TO GET LAID.

SO I YELL,
"WHAT WILL IT BE LADS? THE FIRST ROUND'S ON ME!"
BUT NO MATTER WHAT THEY CHOOSE,
IT'LL BE TURNED INTO PEE.

SO THEY ALL SHOUT BACK *"FOSTERS!"*
AND IT'S OFF TO THE BAR.
BUT GOOD LUCK GETTING SERVED,
WHEN THE QUEUE TRAILS THAT FAR.

SO I JUST WAVE MY MONEY,
AND POLITELY WAIT FOR MY TURN.
AND THEN SOME ARSEHOLE BUTTS IN,
AND CAUSES ME CONCERN.

SO I THINK, *"WHAT'S WITH THIS JERK!"*
"DOESN'T HE SEE THE QUEUE?"
AND TO MAKE MATTERS EVEN WORSE,
THE GIRL BEHIND THE BAR IS SERVING HIM, TOO!

AND THIS DRIVES ME EVEN CRAZIER,
AND I THINK, *"THIS MUST BE STOPPED!"*
BUT THEN I REALISE THAT HE'S SIX-SIX,
AND I'M AFRAID TO BE BOPPED.

SO I GO BACK TO WAITING,
WHILE I QUIETLY FUME.
SECRETLY HOPING I'M NOT THE LAST PERSON,
TO BE SERVED IN THE ROOM.

BUT I EVENTUALLY GET BACK TO MY TABLE,
WITH A TRAY FULL OF DRINKS.
WHERE ALL MY MATES JEER AND TELL ME
THAT MY CRAP SERVICE STINKS.

SO THE FIRST ROUND GOES DOWN QUICKLY,
FOLLOWED BY ROUNDS TWO AND THREE.
AND THEN SOME BRIGHT SPARK SHOUTS,
"LET'S GO FOR A CURRY!"

AND THIS IDEA IS QUICKLY LIKED,
AND INITIATES THE CHUGGING OF BOOZE.
BUT BEFORE WE ALL LEAVE,
THERE'S A MAD DASH FOR THE LOOS.

SO NOW WE'RE ALL CHANTING *"CURRY! CURRY! CURRY!"*
AS WE LURCH DOWN THE STREET.
BUT AT THE RESTAURANT DOOR,
OUR BOORISH BEHAVIOUR DENIES US A SEAT.

AND THIS OUTCOME IS MUCH UNEXPECTED,
AND OUR HEARTS HIT THE FLOOR.
AND THEN SOMEONE SHOUTS,
"LET'S FIND THE NEAREST BAR AND ORDER ROUND NUMBER
FOUR!"

Forgetful Musician:

Felix was a forgetful musician from Poughkeepsie
who went out drinking and got very tipsy.
    So he called on his cell for an *Uber*,
    who refused to transport him and his tuba,
so he had to settle instead for getting a gypsy.

(This only makes sense if my understanding of how to pronounce Poughkeepsie properly is correct [per-kip-see] and that you also have some knowledge of the existence of gypsy cabs operating within the U.S.; otherwise this limerick is basically up shit creek without a paddle and about as funny as a fart in a packed lift.)

LUCOZADE

WHO DO *LUCOZADE* THINK THEY'RE BLOODY KIDDING,
WITH ALL THIS NEW REBRANDING SHIT?
AND I DON'T KNOW ABOUT YOU, OF COURSE,
BUT I AIN'T FUCKING BUYING ANY OF IT.

YOU SEE, *LUCOZADE* ISN'T FOR SPORTSPEOPLE
IT'S FOR THOSE WHO ARE SICK.
OR FOR THOSE GETTING OVER HANGOVERS,
WHOSE HEADS ARE FEELING THICK!

Alcoholic Priest:

Unfortunately, Father Donovan really loved to get pissed,
which led to many of the priest's services being missed.
So he prayed to his Lord and Saviour
to curb his drunken behaviour,
but got bloody nowhere because God doesn't exist.

ILLNESS

I'M SHIVERING AND SWEATING,
AND I JUST WANT TO DIE.
AS I'VE CONTRACTED AN ILLNESS,
NOT THAT I KNOW HOW OR WHY.

AND MAYBE I GOT IT FROM THE KIDS,
OR PICKED UP SOME BUG AT WORK.
OR FROM THE GUY WHO SNEEZED ON THE BUS,
THAT STUPID FUCKING JERK.

SO I'M WRAPPED UP IN A DUVET,
AND TUCKED UP IN BED.
AND THE DRUGS AREN'T WORKING,
JUDGING BY MY STILL POUNDING HEAD.

IT ALSO SMELLS LIKE MY GUTS ARE ROTTING,
AND THE ODOUR REALLY OFFENDS.
AND I FEAR I'LL SOON BE EVACUATING STUFF
SIMULTANEOUSLY FROM BOTH ENDS.

SO I DON'T THINK I'LL MAKE IT TO THE BATHROOM,
AND LIE DOWN WITH A BOWL.
AND I WOULD GIVE ABSOLUTELY ANYTHING TO FEEL BETTER,
EVEN MY SOUL.

AND I'D MAKE A SWIFT DEAL WITH THE DEVIL
IN A RAPID HEARTBEAT.
IN ORDER TO GET OVER THIS ILLNESS,
AND GET BACK ON MY FEET.

SO MY PARTNER THINKS IT'S THE MAN-FLU,
BUT I FEEL IT'S MUCH MORE.
AS MY GUTS, THROAT AND ANUS
ARE ALL TERRIBLY SORE.

SO I ASK HER TO RING THE DOCTOR,
AND SHE SIMPLY LAUGHS IN MY FACE.
AND THEN I PROJECTILE VOMIT
ALL OVER THE SHARED LIVING SPACE.

SO MY PARTNER FINALLY PHONES THE DOCTOR,
BUT HIS ARRIVAL TAKES QUITE A WHILE.
AND BY THE TIME HE EVENTUALLY GETS TO ME,
I'M FAR TOO ILL TO FAKE A SMILE.

AND THEN THE DOC PRODS ME AND POKES ME,
AND EVEN LOOKS DOWN MY THROAT.
AND I HAPPILY PAY BACK HIS TARDINESS,
BY PUKING ALL OVER HIS COAT!

ROYAL BABY

A NEW ROYAL BABY WAS BORN IN 2015
FOR PROUD PARENTS WILLIAM AND KATE.
WHO POPPED OUT AT 8 POUNDS AND 3 OUNCES,
WHICH WAS A VERY DECENT WEIGHT.

AND THEIR DAUGHTER WAS BORN AT 8:35 A.M.,
ON THE SECOND DAY OF MAY.
AND, GIVEN SHE WAS PERFECTLY HEALTHY,
THERE'S NOTHING MORE TO SAY.

NOW, SOME LANDMARKS WERE ILLUMINATED IN PINK,
TO MARK THE ROYAL BIRTH.
WHICH BRIGHTENED LONDON'S SKYLINE,
AND ADDED SOME CITYWIDE MIRTH.

AND SOME GUNS WERE EVEN FIRED,
JUST TWO DAYS LATER.
WHEN CHARLOTTE ELIZABETH DIANA,
WAS NAMED BY HER PARENTAL CREATOR.

AND CHARLOTTE'S WORTH AN ESTIMATED 3-BILLION QUID,
WHICH IS AN INTERESTING THING.
AS THAT'S FAR MORE THAN HER OLDER BROTHER GEORGE,
WHO COULD ONE DAY BE KING.

AND THIS WAS DUBBED AS THE "CHARLOTTE EFFECT"
AT LEAST, THAT'S WHAT THE PRESS WROTE.
SO WE SHOULD ALL THANK THE YOUNG PRINCESS,
FOR KEEPING THE BRITISH ECONOMY AFLOAT!

Infertile Woman:

Irene was an infertile woman from Gloucester
who wanted some children to foster.
    So she took out a large ad
    despite her husband claiming she was mad
and now she's got a full bloody roster.

BLACK COFFEE

THIS IS ONE OF THE WEIRDER 2015 NEWS ITEMS,
THAT I DECIDED TO PICK.
AND GIVEN ITS RATHER DISTURBING NATURE,
IT'LL BE OVER QUITE QUICK.

AND WE CAN THANK RESEARCHERS IN AUSTRIA,
FOR BRINGING US THIS STORY.
BUT THEIR TEST GROUP WAS SO SMALL,
THAT IT WON'T EARN THEM MUCH GLORY.

SO THEY EXAMINED THEIR SUBJECTS' TASTE PREFERENCES,
BUT THEY DIDN'T STOP THERE.
AS THEY ALSO MADE THEM FILL OUT
A PERSONALITY QUESTIONNAIRE.

AND THIS REVEALED THAT BLACK COFFEE DRINKERS
ARE MORE LIKELY TO BE PSYCHOPATHS.
AND I TOLD YOU THIS STORY WAS DARK,
AND UNWORTHY OF LAUGHS.

AND I'M A BLACK COFFEE DRINKER MYSELF,
SO I CAN CONFIRM THAT THIS IS TRUE.
ONLY JOKING! I'M ACTUALLY ALLERGIC TO MILK,
SO I'M JUST SCREWING WITH YOU.

BUT THE NEXT TIME YOU'RE OUT ON A DATE, THOUGH,
YOU SHOULD CHECK YOUR DATE'S COFFEE ORDER.
JUST TO MAKE SURE YOU'RE NOT OUT WITH SOMEONE
WHO HAS A PSYCHOPATHIC DISORDER!

Poor Linda:

This is the gruesome tale of a poor woman called Linda
who unfortunately met a cannibal via *Tinder*.
    She declared him an unsuitable mate
    after just one date,
so he followed her to her home and skinned 'er.

PEPPER BOT

PEPPER IS THE FIRST SUCCESSFUL HOME ROBOT
TO BE BUILT, SOLD AND ADOPTED IN JAPAN.
BUT I'M SURE THEY'LL BE SHIPPING HIM OVERSEAS
JUST AS FAST AS THEY HUMANLY CAN.

AND HE'S ALSO BEEN PLACED IN ALL THE BRANCHES
OF A VERY LARGE JAPANESE BANK.
AND I KNOW WHAT YOU'RE PROBABLY THINKING,
BUT THIS ISN'T SOME SILLY PRANK.

NOW, UNLIKE THE ROBOTS BEFORE HIM,
PEPPER WASN'T BUILT FOR DOMESTIC USE.
HE WAS DESIGNED SOLELY AS A COMPANION,
TO HELP KEEP PEOPLE HAPPY AND LOOSE.

AND ALTHOUGH HE'S A HUMAN-SHAPED ROBOT,
HE DOESN'T HAVE ANY LEGS OR KNEES.
BUT HE ONLY COSTS A THOUSAND POUNDS,
ALBEIT WITH SOME HEFTY MONTHLY FEES.

NOW, ACCORDING TO HIS MAKERS,
PEPPER'S KINDLY, ENDEARING AND EVEN SURPRISING.
THOUGH, I'M SURE HE'LL BE THE FIRST TO KILL US
IF THERE'S EVER A ROBOTIC UPRISING.

AND HE'S ALSO CAPABLE OF PERCEIVING
OUR REAL HUMAN EMOTIONS.
SO HE CAN QUICKLY ADAPT HIS BEHAVIOUR,
BASED ON OUR TANTRUMS AND COMMOTIONS.

AND PEPPER CAN ALSO RECOGNISE HUMAN FACES,
SPEAK, HEAR AND MOVE AROUND.
BUT HE'S NOT PARTICULARLY FAST, HOWEVER,
AT ACTUALLY COVERING A LOT OF GROUND.

AND HE CAN ALSO BE PERSONALISED WITH DOWNLOADS,
SO HE CAN PLAY GAMES AND EVEN DANCE.
BUT BEFORE YOU GET ANY WEIRD IDEAS, MY FRIEND,
HE WASN'T BUILT TO HANDLE ROMANCE!

UNDERPANTS

I PREFER WEARING UNDERPANTS TO BOXER SHORTS,
AND HERE'S THE REASON WHY.
BECAUSE THEY ACT AS A MUCH BETTER DRIP-TRAY,
AFTER I'VE ZIPPED UP MY FLY.

AND I'M SURE THERE ARE MANY GUYS
WHO'D BACK ME UP ON THIS.
AS UNDERPANTS ARE MUCH BETTER
AT ABSORBING THOSE STRAY DRIBBLES OF PISS.

AND I CAN ALSO THINK OF ANOTHER REASON,
AFTER A MOMENT OF REFLECTION.
AS THEY'RE ALSO MUCH BETTER AT DISGUISING
A BLOKE'S UNWANTED ERECTION.

NOT THAT I EVER HAVE THAT PROBLEM, OF COURSE,
NOT WITH MY MICRO-DICK.
BUT I'M SURE IT'S ANOTHER VALID REASON
WHY THEY'RE MOST GUYS' UNDERWEAR PICK.

AND THEN THERE ARE SKID MARKS, AS WELL,
NOT THAT THEY'RE RELEVANT TO ME.
AS I'M A VERY LIBERAL WIPER,
SO MY UNDERPANTS ARE SHIT FREE.

BUT I'M SURE THERE ARE LOTS OF GUYS OUT THERE,
WHO DON'T WIPE AS WELL AS THEY SHOULD.
WHICH IS WHY ALL THEIR UNDERPANTS,
LOOK LIKE THEY'VE BEEN STAINED WITH DAMP WOOD.

AND IF ALL THESE REASONS AREN'T GOOD ENOUGH,
THEN LET ME GIVE YOU ONE MORE.
AS THEY'RE ALSO GREAT AT STOPPING UNWANTED DRAFTS
FROM INVADING MY BACKDOOR!

Micropenis Syndrome:

I've got a very good friend called Jerome
who also suffers from micropenis syndrome.
His dick is so bloody small
his new wife's never seen it at all,
which is why she's chucking him out of their home.

WEEKENDS

TWO DAYS SEEMS LIKE AN AWFULLY LONG TIME,
'TIL YOU CONVERT IT INTO FORTY-EIGHT HOURS.
AND A GREAT DEAL OF THOSE'LL BE SPENT SLEEPING,
AND TAKING SEVERAL, LENGTHY HOT SHOWERS.

AND THEN YOU'LL NEED TO EAT AND DRINK REGULARLY, TOO,
AND DO SOME BORING BLOODY CHORES.
AND IF YOU HAPPEN TO BE A SPORTS FAN,
THEN YOU'LL NEED TO TRACK YOUR FAVOURITE TEAM'S SCORES.

SO YOU'LL PROBABLY HAVE TO WASH THE CAR AFTER THAT,
AND THEN MOW THE FUCKING LAWN.
AND YOU'LL HAVE TO FOLLOW THAT WITH SOME LAUNDRY,
AS ALL YOUR CLEAN UNDIES HAVE BEEN WORN.

THEN YOU MIGHT HAVE TO GO GROCERY SHOPPING, TOO,
WHICH IS NEVER MUCH FUN.
AND BELIEVE IT OR NOT, MY FRIEND,
YOU'RE STILL A LONG WAY FROM BEING DONE.

SO NEXT, YOU'LL HAVE TO POP INTO THE OFFICE,
OR DO ALL THE WORK YOU'VE BROUGHT HOME.
AND ONLY ONCE THAT NIGHTMARE'S BEEN COMPLETED,
WILL YOU FINALLY BE FREE TO ROAM.

SO NOW YOU CAN CATCH-UP WITH ALL YOUR MATES,
AND HAVE A FEW DRINKS AND A CHAT.
BUT YOU'LL HAVE TO BE FAIRLY QUICK, THOUGH,
AS YOU'VE STILL GOT SOME DIY TO DO AFTER THAT.

AND IF YOU THOUGHT DOING DIY WAS A DRAG,
IT'S GOT NOTHING ON VISITING YOUR FOLKS.
WHICH IS PRECIOUS TIME YOU'LL NEVER GET BACK,
AND MORE THE STUFF OF NIGHTMARES THAN JOKES.

AND BY NOW YOU'VE NEGLECTED YOUR PARTNER,
SO YOU'LL HAVE TO APOLOGISE WITH SOME FLOWERS.
WHICH IS WHEN YOU REALISE YOUR TWO DAYS OF FREE TIME,
HAS BEEN REDUCED TO JUST A COUPLE OF HOURS!

SMELLY FEET

YOU MAY THINK THIS IS A FORM OF B.O.,
BUT THE TWO DEFINITELY AREN'T THE SAME.
HENCE THE NEED FOR A SEPARATE RHYME,
WITH A COMPLETELY DIFFERENT NAME.

NOW, I DON'T HAVE SMELLY FEET MYSELF,
BUT I'VE GOT A FRIEND WHO ACTUALLY DOES.
AND HIS DOGS RELEASE A DEADLY VAPOUR,
WHICH GIVES YOU AN UNPLEASANT BUZZ.

AND MY MATE'S A VERY GOOD-LOOKING GUY,
WHO ATTRACTS WOMEN IN THEIR FLOCKS.
BUT THEY SOON RUN THE OTHER WAY,
WHEN HE REMOVES HIS SHOES AND SOCKS.

AND AT FIRST, THERE'S JUST A WHIFF,
LIKE THE SMELL OF OVERRIPE CHEESE.
THEN IT'S JOINED BY A NOXIOUS GAS,
WHICH HINTS AT A SERIOUS DISEASE.

AND MY FRIEND'S A REALLY FUN GUY,
AND HE'S ALSO AS SMART A WHIP.
BUT YOU WOULDN'T WANT TO SHARE HIS ROOM
ON A LENGTHY BUSINESS TRIP.

AND AS WELL AS ALL HIS LUGGAGE,
HE TRAVELS WITH SOME CLEAN PLASTIC BAGS.
SO THE STENCH FROM HIS REEKING SOCKS
CAN'T INFECT HIS OTHER WEARABLE RAGS.

AND, SADLY, GIVEN THAT MY MATE'S FAIRLY OLD NOW,
I DOUBT HE'LL EVER FIND A CURE.
SO HE'LL JUST HAVE TO LIVE WITH THE GLOOMY FACT
THAT HIS FEET SMELL LIKE MANURE!

Successful Businessman:

There was a successful businessman named Pete
whose wonderful life was still incomplete.
He had the looks and the money,
was also charming and funny,
but couldn't attract a wife due to his foul-smelling feet.

OCD

I THINK WE ALL DEAL WITH SOME DEGREE OF OCD,
THOUGH, IN MOST IT'S VERY MILD.
AND I'M CERTAINLY NO EXCEPTION,
AND HAVE HAD MY IMPULSES SINCE I WAS A CHILD.

AND I'M NOT A COMPULSIVE CLEANER,
OR EVEN OBSESSED WITH BEING OVERLY NEAT.
BUT I DO LIKE THINGS TO BE ORGANISED,
SO I'M NOT THE MOST DISORDERLY PERSON YOU'LL EVER MEET.

NOW, AS FOR MY OWN COMPULSIVE DISORDERS,
I'M ONLY GOING TO DISCUSS A FEW.
AND THE FIRST OF THOSE IS COFFEE,
WHICH IS GIVING YOU A SERIOUSLY BIG CLUE.

SO I HAVE TO STIR EVERY MUG OF COFFEE I MAKE,
EXACTLY TWENTY-FOUR TIMES.
AND NOW I'VE RHYMED MYSELF INTO A CORNER,
WHICH IS THE LEAST OF MY CRIMES.

SO LET'S MOVE ON TO WINE GUMS, INSTEAD,
WHICH I HAVE TO EAT IN COLOUR ORDER.
AND I KNOW THAT THAT'S CROSSING A LINE,
BUT AT LEAST I'M NOT A HOARDER.

THOUGH, I DO HAVE A LARGE DVD COLLECTION,
WHICH I'VE MENTIONED IN THE PAST.
AND WHEN I SAY THAT IT'S LARGE,
I'M TALKING EXTREMELY, HUGELY, VAST.

SO THAT'S THE END OF THE MILD STUFF, THEN,
AND NOW IT'S TIME TO TAKE IT UP A NOTCH.
AND I'M NOT TALKING ABOUT THE NUMEROUS TIMES
THAT I PLAY WITH MY OWN CROTCH.

I'M ACTUALLY TALKING ABOUT WHEN I GO OUT WALKING,
AND COUNTING THE STEPS THAT I TAKE.
BUT IT'S NOT FREAKING ME OUT YET,
AND IT'S NOT KEEPING ME AWAKE.

AND WHAT OF MY NAIL BITING OR NOSE PICKING,
AND THEN THERE'S SUCKING MY THUMB.
BUT THOSE THINGS SEEM MORE LIKE BAD HABITS,
SO I THINK I'LL KEEP SCHTUM!

FEVER

I'M SWEATING MY TITS OFF,
AND MY TEMPERATURE'S A HUNDRED-AND-ONE.
SO FEEL FREE TO STICK A FORK IN ME,
BECAUSE I THINK THAT I'M DONE.

AND I WENT TO BED FEELING FINE,
AND WOKE UP FEELING LIKE SHIT.
AS WELL AS HAVING THE SENSATION,
OF BEING ROASTED IN A BARBECUE PIT.

SO I MAKE A QUICK CALL IN TO WORK,
TO EXPLAIN THAT I'M FEELING UNDER THE WEATHER.
AND I ALSO MENTION THAT I'M TERRIBLY WEAK,
AND COULD BE KNOCKED DOWN BY A FEATHER.

AND MY BOSS TELLS ME TO TAKE IT EASY,
AND NOT TO RETURN 'TIL I'M READY.
BUT I PROMISE HIM I'LL BE BACK SOON,
ONCE I'M FEELING MORE STEADY.

BUT ALL MY TALK IS JUST BRAVADO, THOUGH,
AS MY FEVER SWIFTLY GETS WORSE.
AND I SOON FIND MYSELF SLIPPING AWAY
INTO A WHOLE 'NOTHER UNIVERSE.

A PLACE THAT'S FULL OF FEVERISH NIGHTMARES,
AND DARK, DELIRIOUS DREAMS.
WHERE NOTHING IS REAL,
OR WHAT IT ACTUALLY SEEMS.

SO THERE'S NOTHING ELSE I CAN DO NOW,
BUT JUST LIE HERE AND SWEAT.
WHILE THE FEVER RAVAGES MY BODY,
AND I BECOME MORE AND MORE WET.

SO I CURL UP INTO A BALL,
AND PRAY IT'LL BE OVER REAL QUICK.
WHILE I SHIVER BENEATH MY DUVET,
AND TRY NOT TO BE SICK!

RESOLUTIONS

I'VE NEVER MADE A NEW YEAR'S RESOLUTION MYSELF.
NOT ONCE IN MY LIFE.
BECAUSE I KNOW I'D NEVER FUCKING KEEP IT,
SO WHY BOTHER WITH THE STRIFE.

AND I DON'T WANT TO QUIT SMOKING,
OR TO REDUCE MY INTAKE OF BOOZE.
SO NOT MAKING ANY RESOLUTIONS
SEEMED THE MUCH SANER OPTION TO CHOOSE.

AND I SEE PEOPLE EATING SALAD AT WORK,
AS PART OF THEIR POST-XMAS CLEANSE.
LIKE CONSUMING SOME RAW VEGETABLES,
WILL SUDDENLY MAKE AMENDS.

AND THEY'VE BEEN STUFFING THEMSELVES STUPID,
FOR AT LEAST A FUCKING WEEK.
SO EATING RABBIT FOOD FOR A FEW DAYS
ISN'T GOING TO MAKE THEM MAGICALLY SLEEK.

AND WHAT ABOUT ALL THOSE PEOPLE, TOO,
WHO PROMISE THAT THEY'LL GO TO THE GYM.
AND THEY EVEN BUY AN EXPENSIVE MEMBERSHIP,
SO IT'S NOT PERCEIVED AS A WHIM.

BUT THEY ONLY MANAGE A FEW VISITS, THOUGH,
BEFORE THEY LOSE THE DESIRE.
WHICH IS EQUIVALENT TO TOSSING WADS OF CASH
ONTO A ROARING OPEN FIRE.

AND DON'T GET ME FUCKING STARTED
WITH ALL THAT SELF-IMPROVEMENT CRAP.
SUCH AS, DOING AN ONLINE DEGREE
TO BRIDGE AN EDUCATIONAL GAP.

AND AFTER GETTING HOME FROM WORK,
I DON'T WANT TO SIT DOWN AND STUDY.
I WANT TO WATCH SOME TV INSTEAD,
OR GO OUT DRINKING WITH A BUDDY.

AND THEN THERE'S MONEY MANAGEMENT, OF COURSE,
AND TRYING TO REDUCE MY DEBT.
BUT I'D MUCH RATHER POP DOWN TO THE BOOKIES,
AND PLACE THE ODD BET.

AND I'LL FINISH BY TELLING YOU THE REASON,
WHY MOST PEOPLE FAIL TO REACH THEIR GOALS.
BECAUSE THEY ALWAYS SET SUCH UNACHIEVABLE TARGETS,
THE POOR DELUDED SOULS!

FAVOURITE MOVIE?

WHEN SOMEONE ENQUIRES ABOUT MY FAVOURITE MOVIE,
I HAVE TO QUESTION THEIR SANITY.
FOLLOWED BY AN "ARE YOU FUCKING KIDDING ME?" LOOK,
AND A LIBERAL DOSE OF PROFANITY.

AND I'VE WATCHED A MILLION GREAT FILMS,
AND HAVE A VAST DVD COLLECTION.
SO HOW AM I SUPPOSED TO POINT TO JUST ONE,
AND CLAIM IT'S CINEMATIC PERFECTION?

YOU SEE, THIS NOTION IS ABSURD TO ME,
JUST LIKE THE STUPID FUCKING QUESTION.
AS I COULD NEVER SELECT JUST ONE;
I COULDN'T EVEN MAKE A TENTATIVE SUGGESTION.

AND EVEN IF THEY TOOK A LOADED GUN,
AND STUCK IT TO MY BAFFLED HEAD.
I STILL WOULDN'T CHOOSE A MOVIE,
AND THEY'D HAVE TO SHOOT ME DEAD.

AND, SURE, I HAVE MY FAVOURITES,
LIKE MY FAVOURITE BEER, BISCUIT OR SNACK.
BUT HAVING TO SELECT JUST ONE FILM
WOULD CAUSE ME TO HAVE A PANIC ATTACK.

AND EVEN NAMING MY TOP TEN,
WOULD BE A VERY DIFFICULT SHOUT.
BECAUSE I'D SECRETLY BE STRESSING,
THAT I'D LEFT SOMETHING OUT.

AND THE MORE THAT I THINK ABOUT THIS,
THE MORE MADDER I GET.
AS I CAN'T WRAP MY HEAD AROUND IT,
AND IT'S MAKING ME UPSET.

SO DO ME A FAVOUR, MY FRIEND,
AND NEVER ASK ANYONE TO PICK.
BECAUSE, THIS QUESTION ISN'T FAIR;
IT'S JUST UTTERLY EVIL AND SICK!

HAIRCUT

I LOATHE GETTING MY HAIR CUT ONCE A MONTH,
AS I'VE NEVER GOT ANYTHING TO SAY.
I JUST WANT TO GET MY HEAD SHEARED IN SILENCE,
AND THEN JUST QUIETLY PAY.

BUT I GET PEPPERED WITH ANNOYING QUESTIONS,
ESPECIALLY ABOUT HOLIDAYS AND WORK.
AND AS I'M TOTALLY SHIT AT SMALL TALK,
THEY DRIVE ME FUCKING BERSERK.

AND I ALWAYS GO TO A TRADITIONAL GENTS' BARBER,
TO TRY AND ERADICATE THE YAP.
BUT I STILL CAN'T FIND SOMEONE TO CUT MY HAIR,
WHILST ALSO SHUTTING THEIR TRAP.

AND THEY NATTER ABOUT THE WEATHER,
AND ALL SORTS OF TEDIOUS BLOODY SPORT.
AND AS I'M COMPLETELY USELESS AT CHITCHAT,
I DON'T HAVE ANY SENSIBLE RETORT.

AND I KNOW WHAT YOU'RE THINKING NOW.
WHY DON'T I JUST LET MY HAIR GROW?
BUT HAVE YOU EVER SEEN AN OLD, SKINNY, WHITE DUDE
WITH A CRAZY AFRO!

NECTAR POINTS

NOW, I'M NOT ANGRY ABOUT GETTING NECTAR POINTS,
AS I LOVE A GOOD REWARD.
BUT I AM UPSET BY CLASHING COUPONS,
WHICH PROVES THAT SAINSBURY'S SYSTEM IS FLAWED.

AND I'LL BE GIVEN TWO BONUS COUPONS QUITE OFTEN,
WHICH DO EXACTLY THE SAME THING.
BUT I'LL ONLY BE ALLOWED TO REDEEM ONE OF THEM,
WHICH IS THE ANNOYING FUCKING STING.

AND WHY DOES THE STUPID TILL SPIT THEM OUT,
WHEN THEY'RE OBVIOUSLY GOING TO CLASH?
AND WHY ISN'T IT CLEVER ENOUGH NOT TO,
GIVEN IT'S CAPABLE OF TAKING MY BLOODY CASH.

AND I JUST HAVE TO STAND THERE QUIETLY, OF COURSE,
AND THEN PAY THE SODDING BILL.
WHILE I FANTASISE ABOUT GRABBING A BASEBALL BAT,
AND SMASHING UP THE FUCKING TILL!

NEEDLESS NOISE

I HAVE HYPER-SENSITIVE HEARING,
WHICH IS WHY I REALLY HATE NEEDLESS NOISE.
SO ANY UNWANTED REPETITIVE SOUND,
IS LIKELY TO HAVE ME THROWING OUT MY TOYS.

AND IT COULD QUITE LITERALLY BE ANYTHING,
LIKE A DRAFTY, RATTLING DOOR.
OR SOME STORMY WHISTLING WINDOWS
OR AN OLD CREAKING FLOOR.

AND ANY DRIPPING TAP OR SHOWER
WILL ALSO QUICKLY OFFEND.
BUT IT'S THE UNNECESSARY HUMAN NOISES,
WHICH REALLY DRIVE ME ROUND THE BEND.

SO LET'S START WITH HUMMING AND WHISTLING,
AND PEOPLE NOT SITTING STILL.
BUT IT'S ALL THOSE FUCKERS TAPPING PENS,
THAT I'D REALLY LIKE TO KILL.

AND IN THESE TIMES WHEN LISTENING TO PERSONAL MUSIC
HAS BECOME SO PROLIFIC.
I FIND THE TINNY SOUND ESCAPING FROM HEADPHONES
IS BORDERING ON HORRIFIC.

AND THEN THERE'S FUCKING CAR ALARMS, TOO,
OR ANY SODDING ALARM, FOR THAT MATTER.
AS THEY ALL PUSH MY BLOODY BUTTONS,
AND CAUSE ME TO EMIT WORDS THAT DON'T FLATTER.

AND DESPITE ALL THE FUN I'M HAVING WITH THIS,
I'M GOING TO QUICKLY WRAP THINGS UP.
BY STATING THAT MY MOST ANNOYING NOISE OF ALL
IS SOME ARSEHOLE SLURPING FROM A CUP!

Ex-NASCAR Driver:

There was a disgraced ex-NASCAR driver called Russ
who was forced to drive a school bus.
He hated the noisy kids
and the lack of skids
and despised not being able to cuss.

DRIVING

DRIVING USED TO MEAN FREEDOM,
AND TRAVELLING TO PLACES FOR FUN.
BUT NOW IT'S ALL ABOUT LENGTHY QUEUING,
AND AN AVERAGE MILES-PER-HOUR OF ONE.

AND CARS HAVE BECOME MUCH BETTER AND SAFER,
AND FASTER BY MANY MILES.
JUST SO THEY CAN BE STACKED ON OUR HIGHWAYS
IN PRETTY, MULTI-COLOURED PILES.

AND I REMEMBER COLLECTING MY MATES AT THE WEEKEND,
AND DRIVING THEM TO THE COAST.
BUT NOW WE JUST SIT AROUND AND PLAY DRIVING GAMES
THAT ALLOW US TO BOAST.

AND I'M NOT SURE I'D MISS DRIVING NOW,
GIVEN THE INCREASING ROAD RAGE.
WHERE NORMAL PEOPLE BECOME WILD ANIMALS,
JUST RELEASED FROM A CAGE.

AND IT'S NOT JUST THE RISE IN ROAD VIOLENCE,
THAT WE ACTUALLY NEED TO CONSIDER.
AS THERE'S AVOIDING ALL THE CASH-MAKING SPEED CAMERAS,
BEING ERECTED BY THE LOWEST BIDDER.

AND WHAT OF THE LEARNER DRIVERS, TAXIS, BUSES,
AND ALL THE GUYS IN WHITE VANS.
NOT TO MENTION THE MASSES OF MISDIRECTED OLD PEOPLE,
WHO AREN'T MAKING ANY FANS.

BUT THIS ALL SEEMS QUITE NEGATIVE, THOUGH,
SO MAYBE WE SHOULD LOOK FOR SOME DRIVING TREASURE.
BUT WE CAN'T EVEN DRIVE INTO A CITY NOW,
WITHOUT BEING CHARGED FOR THE BLOODY PLEASURE.

AND WE HAVEN'T EVEN DISCUSSED YET,
ALL THE FUEL THAT WE USE AND POUR.
THE EVER SOARING PRICES OF WHICH,
IS LIKE A SERIOUS PUNCH TO THE JAW.

AND IT WOULD BE REMISS OF ME TO FINISH,
WITHOUT MENTIONING A CONTINUING FARCE.
I'M TALKING ABOUT ALL THE DANGEROUS BOY RACERS,
WHO'RE A TOTAL PAIN IN THE ARSE.

SO, IS IT REALLY WORTH DRIVING THESE DAYS,
GIVEN THAT THERE ARE SO VERY FEW PERKS?
AND WHEN WAS THE LAST TIME YOU HAD A MAJOR JOURNEY,
THAT WAS DEVOID OF FUCKING ROADWORKS!

SCHOOL

FROM THE AGES OF FOUR TO SIXTEEN,
WE BLINDLY FOLLOW THE RULES.
WHILE WE STRUGGLE WITH ADOLESCENCE,
AND NAVIGATE FOUR OR FIVE SCHOOLS.

AND IT ALL STARTS WITH PLAYSCHOOL,
AFTER WE'VE JUST LEARNT TO WALK AND TALK.
THE FIRST PLACE WHERE OUR PARENTS GLADLY DUMP US,
SO THEY CAN'T HEAR US SQUAWK.

SO, INFANTS SCHOOL COMES NEXT, THEN,
NOT THAT IT REALLY MATTERS.
AS ALL OUR TIME'S SPENT COLOURING THINGS IN,
AND REDUCING OUR NEW CLOTHES TO TATTERS.

AND PRIMARY SCHOOL IS AFTER THAT,
THOUGH, IT'S JUST REALLY MORE OF THE SAME.
BUT AT LEAST WE LEARN THE ALPHABET,
AND HOW TO READ AND WRITE OUR OWN NAME.

SO, SECONDARY SCHOOL IS LAST,
WHICH IS BASICALLY FIVE YEARS OF TORTUROUS HELL.
WHERE OUR NARCISSISTIC, CONTROL FREAK TEACHERS,
EXPECT US TO DO MUCH MORE THAN JUST SPELL.

AND THEY PUSH US REALLY HARD FROM NINE TO FIVE,
WHICH IS EIGHT HOURS A DAY.
JUST SO THAT WE CAN JOIN THEM IN THE RAT RACE,
OF WORK, REST AND PLAY.

BUT WE DO GET AN HOUR FOR LUNCH, THOUGH,
WHICH CAN'T COME TOO SOON.
UNLESS YOU GET STUCK SITTING NEXT TO THE KID,
WHO GOUGES OUT HIS EYE WITH A SPOON.

AND WHAT OF ALL THE CORE SUBJECTS,
THAT WE WERE FORCED TO MENTALLY DIGEST.
AS THERE WAS MATHS, ENGLISH AND THE SCIENCES,
THOUGH, ART WAS USUALLY THE BEST.

SO, THERE ARE SOME THINGS WE HAVEN'T COVERED,
LIKE PHYSICAL EDUCATION AND SPORT.
NOT THAT MISSING THESE TIME WASTERS
AFFECTED OUR END OF YEAR REPORT.

AND THEN THERE WAS KISSING, OF COURSE,
AND SMOKING BEHIND THE BIKE SHEDS.
NOT TO MENTION, STRESSING OUT OUR TEACHERS,
UNTIL THEY NEEDED TO TAKE MEDS!

PIZZA

WHEN DID GOING OUT FOR A PIZZA,
BECOME MORE ABOUT EATING BLOODY SALAD?
OR CHOMPING ON PASTA FOR CHRIST'S SAKE,
WHICH IS JUST AS INVALID.

AND EVEN ORDERING-IN THESE DAYS,
HAS BECOME A SERIOUS FUCKING JOKE.
AS THEY TEMPT US TO SPEND MORE MONEY,
BY OFFERING A FREE BOTTLE OF COKE.

AND I STILL REMEMBER THE GOOD OLD DAYS,
THE ONES WITH THE LUNCHTIME BUFFET.
WHERE YOU COULD EAT YOURSELF STUPID,
AND WITH JUST FIVE POUNDS TO PAY.

BUT I DOUBT *PIZZA HUT* DOES THAT ANYMORE,
GIVEN HOW HEALTH CONSCIOUS WE'VE BECOME.
NOT TO MENTION ALL THE PRESSURE WE'RE PUT UNDER,
TO WATCH THE SIZE OF OUR TUM.

AND I KNOW THAT I'M A MISERABLE OLD FART,
AND THAT I SHOULDN'T MOAN SO MUCH.
BUT I'M A MEAT-EATING CARNIVORE,
AND NOT A RABBIT IN A HUTCH.

BUT IT'S NOT ALL BAD NEWS, HOWEVER,
AS THERE'S NOW SO MUCH MORE CHOICE.
SO I THINK I'LL ORDER A LARGE SAUSAGE AND MUSHROOM,
AND REST MY INNER VOICE!

Scottish Lad:

Tommy was a young Scottish lad from Troon
who ate all of his meals with a spoon.
His parents figured it was a whim
and didn't discourage him,
but he's still doing it and he'll be fifty in June.

PETS

I'VE NEVER HAD MUCH LUCK WITH PETS,
AND THAT'S NOT FOR THE WANT OF TRYING.
BUT NO MATTER HOW WELL I LOOKED AFTER THEM,
THEY STILL ENDED UP DYING.

AND I DON'T MEAN FROM OLD AGE, OF COURSE,
BECAUSE THAT SIMPLY WASN'T THE CASE.
AS MOST OF THEM ONLY LASTED A FEW MONTHS,
BEFORE CHECKING-OUT OF THE PET RACE.

SO, I STARTED WITH A SMALL GOLDFISH,
JUST LIKE MOST KIDS PROBABLY DO.
BUT IT ONLY LASTED A FEW WEEKS,
BEFORE BEING FLUSHED DOWN THE LOO.

AND I FOUND IT FLOATING IN ITS BOWL ONE MORNING,
AND JUST THOUGHT THAT IT WAS TIRED.
BUT MY MOTHER SOON INFORMED ME, HOWEVER,
THAT POOR LITTLE GOLDY HAD EXPIRED.

AND I'VE NO IDEA WHY GOLDY DIED,
BUT I SHOULD HAVE HEEDED IT AS A WARNING.
BECAUSE HE WOULDN'T BE THE FIRST PET,
THAT I FOUND DEAD IN THE MORNING.

AND I HAD A BUNCH OF HAMSTERS AFTER THAT,
AND A CUTE LITTLE RABBIT.
AND BURYING MY DECEASED PETS
SOON BECAME A TERRIBLE BURDEN AND HABIT.

BUT I TOOK LOSING FLUFFY REALLY HARD, THOUGH,
AND NEVER GOT ANY MORE PETS.
AND EVEN THOUGH I'VE MISSED THE COMPANIONSHIP,
I DON'T HAVE ANY REGRETS.

AND I WOULD'VE LOVED OWNING A DOG, OF COURSE,
OR EVEN A MORE SELF-RELIANT CAT.
BUT GIVEN MY LETHAL TRACK-RECORD,
I COULDN'T EVEN RISK THAT!

PANIC ATTACK

IT BEGINS WITH A RACING PULSE,
EVEN THOUGH I'M SAT IN A CHAIR.
AND I'VE NO IDEA WHAT STARTED IT,
AS I'VE ONLY JUST BECOME AWARE.

BUT THEN COMES THE RAPID BREATHING,
AND THEN I WORRY ABOUT MY HEART.
AS I KNOW MY GROWING DISCOMFORT,
ISN'T 'COS I'M ABOUT TO LET RIP A FART.

SO NEXT COMES THE DIZZINESS,
AND THEN I GET A REALLY HOT FLASH.
AND NOW'S DEFINITELY NOT THE TIME TO PANIC,
OR DO ANYTHING RASH.

BUT THINGS KEEP GETTING WORSE,
AND THEN I GET A SEVERE SHORTNESS OF BREATH.
WHICH IS WHEN I BEGIN TO CONSIDER,
THAT I MIGHT SOON BE FACING DEATH.

THEN FINALLY, I GET THE CRUSHING PAIN,
LIKE THERE'S AN ELEPHANT SITTING ON MY CHEST.
AND I WONDER IF THIS IS WHAT IT FEELS LIKE
TO HAVE A CARDIAC ARREST.

SO NOW ALL MY SENSES ARE GOING CRAZY,
AND I DON'T KNOW WHAT TO DO.
AND ALTHOUGH I WANT TO CHECK FOR A STROKE,
I DON'T THINK I'LL MAKE IT TO THE LOO.

SO I JUST STAY EXACTLY WHERE I AM,
AND TRY AND GET A GRIP.
AS ALL I CAN REALLY DO NOW
IS HOPE THAT IT'S A RELATIVELY SHORT TRIP.

BUT IT TAKES NEARLY AN HOUR, HOWEVER,
FOR ME NOT TO DIE.
AND ALTHOUGH I SHAT MY PANTS A LITTLE,
I DIDN'T ACTUALLY CRY.

SO EVEN WHEN IT'S OVER,
AND THE PANIC ATTACK HAS FINALLY ABATED.
THE CHEST PAIN STILL LINGERS FOR FUCKING AGES,
WHICH ISN'T UNRELATED.

AS I'M STILL FULL OF ANXIETY, YOU SEE,
AND LOTS OF WORRY AND STRESS.
AND I'M LEFT WONDERING HOW WATCHING TV ALL DAY
GOT ME INTO THIS STUPID BLOODY MESS!

DIARRHOEA

DIARRHOEA IS OBVIOUSLY EMBARRASSING,
AND THEREFORE NO LAUGHING MATTER.
BUT I'M AFRAID THAT NO SUBJECT'S SAFE
FROM MY WARPED, RHYMING PATTER.

AND MY DIARRHOEA COMES ON VERY SWIFTLY,
AND CATCHES ME UNAWARE.
AND THEN FINDING THE NEAREST TOILET
BECOMES MY ONLY REAL CARE.

SO I RUSH INTO THE BATHROOM,
AND QUICKLY TAKE A SEAT.
THEN I PREPARE MYSELF FOR THE NOISE,
AND THE RUSH OF LIQUID HEAT.

AND LET'S NOT FORGET THE SMELL,
SO THANK GOD THAT I'M ALONE.
AS THE AIR ALL AROUND ME
BECOMES AN UNBREATHABLE TOXIC ZONE.

SO MY RING IS SOON CATCHING FIRE,
AND I BLAME THAT LATE NIGHT CURRY.
AND I CURSE MY MATE FOR BRINGING IT ROUND,
SO THANKS A LOT FRIEND MURRAY.

AND I'M SOON SQUIRTING LIQUID SHIT,
AND I CAN'T EVEN WATCH THE TELLY.
AND I CAN KISS GOODBYE TO MY WEEKEND PLANS, TOO,
THANKS TO MY BANGALORE BELLY.

SO NOW I'VE GOT SOME REAL TIME TO KILL,
WHILE I'M GLUED TO THE PORCELAIN THRONE.
AND I DESPERATELY SEARCH ALL MY POCKETS,
HOPING TO FIND MY MOBILE PHONE.

BUT I JUST CAN'T CATCH A BREAK, THOUGH,
AND HAVE TO SETTLE FOR READING A BOOK.
AND AFTER I'VE FINISHED WIPING MY ARSE,
I CAN'T RESIST TAKING A QUICK LOOK.

BUT IT'S NOT A PRETTY SIGHT, HOWEVER,
SO I SHOULD TAKE SOMETHING TO SORT OUT MY GUTS.
BUT I CAN'T FIND ANY FRIGGING *IMODIUM*,
WHICH IS AKIN TO BEING KICKED IN THE NUTS.

AND I'M WORRIED ABOUT LEAVING THE HOUSE,
SO I CONSIDER CALLING MY MUM.
BUT I DON'T RELISH THE THOUGHT OF ADMITTING TO HER,
THAT I'VE GOT A RUNNY BUM!

MUMPS

THE MUMPS IS CONTAGIOUS FOR FIVE DAYS,
AND ONCE CAUGHT, THERE'S NO CURE.
AND IT LASTS FOR ONE TO TWO WEEKS,
WHICH YOU JUST HAVE TO SIT AND ENDURE.

AND IT'S ALSO ONE OF THOSE VIRUSES,
WHICH YOU USUALLY GET AS A KID.
AND I'M SURE I DON'T HAVE TO TELL YOU,
THAT I EVENTUALLY DID.

NOW, I WAS BORN IN THE EARLY '70s,
AND THE M.M.R. VACCINE WAS INTRODUCED IN 1988.
WHICH EXPLAINS WHY I CAUGHT THE MUMPS,
AND HAD TO WATCH MY FACE INFLATE.

AND MUMPS IS VERY PAINFUL,
ESPECIALLY UNDER THE EARS.
AS WAS ALL THE CRUEL NAME-CALLING,
AND THE OTHER KIDS' CONSTANT JEERS.

SO THEY CALLED ME HAMSTER-FACE AND LUMPY,
BECAUSE OF MY FACIAL BUMPS.
AND THEY ALSO TOOK GREAT JOY IN REMINDING ME,
THAT I LOOKED LIKE ONE OF THE FLUMPS.

AND IF YOU'VE NEVER HEARD OF THE FLUMPS,
IT WAS A POPULAR KIDS TV SHOW.
BUT IF YOU WEREN'T AROUND IN THE LATE '70s,
THEN THERE'S NO WAY YOU COULD KNOW!

Weird Little Kid:

Wendell was a weird little kid from Horley
who kept being sick and feeling quite poorly.
    Baffled doctors ran test after test
    at his distressed parents' behest,
while he continued eating the odd creepy-crawly.

119

FERRET

WHEN I HEARD THAT THE QUICKEST EJACULATING ANIMAL,
HAPPENED TO BE THE FERRET.
I WONDERED IF THIS QUIRKY LITTLE FACT
ACTUALLY HAD ANY REAL MERIT.

SO I JUMPED STRAIGHT ONTO *GOOGLE*,
BECAUSE I REALLY NEEDED TO KNOW.
BUT THE RESULT WAS DISAPPOINTING,
AS IT'S ACTUALLY THE MOSQUITO.

AND THEN I OBVIOUSLY WONDERED ABOUT MEN,
AND DECIDED TO TAKE A QUICK LOOK.
SO I LET MY FINGERS DO THE TYPING,
AND CONSULTED THE GUINNESS RECORDS BOOK.

AND I FOUND THAT THE QUICKEST MALE EJACULATION
IS CURRENTLY 12.5 SECONDS.
WHICH, PERSONALLY, SEEMS QUITE LONG,
SO I THINK A NEW FOUND FAME BECKONS!

DEADLY TODDLERS

I IMMEDIATELY CHUCKLED WHEN I SAW THE HEADLINE,
"U.S. TODDLERS SHOOT ONE PERSON A WEEK".
BECAUSE I'VE GOT AN EXTREMELY DARK SOUL,
AND A SERIOUSLY TWISTED HUMOROUS STREAK.

AND THIS COULD ONLY HAPPEN IN AMERICA,
IN THE GUN-TOTING, BIG U. S. OF A.
WHERE THEY LEAVE WEAPONS LYING AROUND THE HOUSE,
WITHOUT CONSIDERING THE PRICE THEY'LL HAVE TO PAY!

Gangsta Rapper:

Triple Threat was a notorious gangsta rapper
who carried a weapon and dressed very dapper.
    Most thought he'd lose his young life
    via a gun or a knife,
but he actually expired on the crapper.

121

INTERNET CONNECTION

SUDDENLY LOSING MY WIRELESS CONNECTION
FILLS ME WITH INDESCRIBABLE RAGE.
AS I'M JUST SAT THERE LIKE A LEMON,
STARING AT A FROZEN WEB PAGE.

AND IF IT OCCURS WHEN I'M PLAYING POKER,
THEN IT COSTS ME FUCKING CASH.
WHICH IS WHEN I REALLY HAVE TO CONTROL MYSELF
NOT TO DO SOMETHING RASH.

AND I PAY A SMALL BLOODY FORTUNE, MIND YOU,
FOR THE LATEST SUPERSONIC SPEED.
BUT MY BROADBAND STILL FUCKING DROPS OUT
AT THE VERY HEIGHT OF MY NEED.

AND THERE'S NO POINT IN COMPLAINING, OF COURSE,
AS MY PROVIDER COULDN'T GIVE A TOSS.
AND THEY'VE COVERED THEIR ARSE WITH SMALL PRINT
BY STATING THEY'RE NOT LIABLE FOR ANY LOSS.

AND WHILE I'M ON THE VERBAL WARPATH,
LET'S DISCUSS THE BLOODY CONNECTION FEE.
WHICH, GIVEN THEY JUST FLICK A FUCKING SWITCH,
SHOULD ALWAYS BE FREE.

BUT WHY WOULD THEY DO US ANY FAVOURS,
WHEN THEY CAN RAPE US FOR MORE MONEY.
AS THEY'RE ALWAYS LOOKING FOR MORE WAYS
OF MAKING THEIR BOTTOM LINES SUNNY.

AND I'D CONSIDER ORGANISING A REVOLT,
TO TEACH ALL THE ISPs A LESSON.
BUT I WOULDN'T LAST A BLOODY WEEK,
WITHOUT MY DAILY SURFING SESSION!

The Internet:

I think that the internet is just bloody fantastic,
as you can buy anything you want, even elastic.
  You can also use it for monkey spanking
  after doing some online banking
and all you need is a small piece of plastic.

COMPUTER VIRUSES

WE'VE GOT TO BE WARY OF ROOTKITS AND MALWARE,
AND EVEN A DEADLY BIOS INFECTION.
WHICH IS WHY WE NEED ANTIVIRUS SOFTWARE,
TO HELP WITH OUR COMPUTER'S PROTECTION.

AND I PAY FOR MY LAPTOP'S SECURITY SOFTWARE,
WHICH COSTS ME SOME CONSIDERABLE CORN.
BUT THEN, I LIKE TO HAVE PEACE OF MIND
WHEN I'M SEARCHING FOR PORN.

AND I HAVE A RIGHT TO LOOK AT PORNOGRAPHY,
WITHOUT MY LAPTOP GETTING SICK.
WHICH IS WHY ALL THE FUCKING COMPUTER VIRUSES,
REALLY GET ON MY WICK.

AND IT DOESN'T MATTER IF IT'S A TROJAN HORSE,
OR A NASTY, MULTI-HEADED WORM.
AS I AUTOMATICALLY HATE ANYTHING THAT INTERFERES
WITH ME RELEASING MY SPERM!

EMPTY CARTONS

FINDING AN EMPTY MILK CARTON IN THE FRIDGE
LEAVES ME QUIVERING WITH RAGE.
AS THERE'S NO FUCKING NEED FOR IT,
NOT IN THIS BLOODY DAY AND AGE.

AND I HAVE TO SLOWLY COUNT TO TEN,
SO I DON'T HUNT DOWN THE OFFENDER.
AS I COULD HAPPILY SHOVE THEIR STUPID HEAD
INSIDE MY NEW *NINJA* BLENDER.

AND IT'S NOT JUST MILK, OF COURSE,
AS THERE ARE FRUIT JUICES AS WELL.
BUT IT'S FINDING AN EMPTY BISCUIT PACKET,
THAT'S MY OWN PERSONAL HELL.

AND THERE'S NOTHING WORSE WHEN I FANCY A *HOBNOB*,
THAN FINDING AN EMPTY FUCKING PACKET.
WHICH IS WHEN I COMPLETELY LOSE MY SHIT,
AS I CAN NO LONGER HACK IT.

SO HERE'S A QUICK MESSAGE FOR ALL THOSE PEOPLE,
WHO ARE COMMITTING THIS TERRIBLE SIN.
STOP BEING SUCH FUCKING ARSEHOLES YOU BASTARDS,
AND PUT YOUR EMPTY CARTONS IN THE BIN!

SELF-CHECKOUT TILLS

SUPERMARKET SELF-CHECKOUT TILLS
SEEM LIKE SUCH A GOOD IDEA.
ESPECIALLY IF I'M JUST NIPPING INSIDE
FOR SOME PIZZA AND BEER.

AND EVEN IF I'VE GOT A BASKET OF ITEMS,
INCLUDING EGGS, MILK AND BREAD.
I CAN STILL SAVE SOME PRECIOUS TIME
BY USING THE SELF-CHECKOUT INSTEAD.

AND THEY'RE ALSO A SERIOUS BOON
FOR THE PURPOSES OF 24-HOUR SHOPPING.
UNTIL THEY GO FUCKING WRONG, OF COURSE,
AND THEN I WANT TO GRAB AN AXE AND START CHOPPING.

AND THERE'S NO SOUND IN THE SUPERMARKET,
THAT'S EVER MORE DREADED OR SCARIER.
THAN WHEN A TILL SUDDENLY BLURTS OUT,
"UNEXPECTED ITEM IN BAGGING AREA."

SO NOW I'M COMPLETELY FUCKED,
AND NEED A REAL PERSON TO COME TO MY AID.
AND WHILE I'M WAITING FOR THEM TO APPEAR,
I LOB THE SMARMY TILL A VERBAL GRENADE.

AND I'M NOT KNOWN FOR MY PATIENCE,
WHEN THINGS DON'T GO TO PLAN.
ESPECIALLY AS I ONLY BLOODY POPPED IN,
TO BUY A NEW FRYING PAN.

SO THE BORED ASSISTANT EVENTUALLY AMBLES OVER,
AND SWIPES THEIR FUCKING CARD.
AND I'M TRYING TO CONTROL MY TEMPER,
WHICH IS BECOMING EXTREMELY HARD.

BUT THEY FIX THE ISSUE BEFORE I EXPLODE, THOUGH,
AND THEN THEY WANDER AWAY.
LEAVING ME SEETHING INSIDE,
AND REGRETTING USING THE SELF-CHECKOUT TODAY!

EXAMS

I'VE GOT SWEATY PALMS,
AND THE PRESSURE IS MOUNTING.
AND ALTHOUGH MY FIRST EXAM AIN'T 'TIL TOMORROW,
THE SECONDS I'M COUNTING.

SO I THINK ABOUT POPPING OUT FOR A DRINK,
AND CONSIDER CALLING MY BUDDY.
BUT THEN I LOSE MY WEAK BOTTLE,
AND JUST STAY AT HOME TO STUDY.

SO, THE EXAM IS VERY NEAR NOW,
AND EVERYONE'S QUEUEING NERVOUSLY OUTSIDE.
AND I'M STILL STUCK IN MY HEAD,
GOING OVER ALL THE RULES I MUST ABIDE.

THEN THE EXAM MODERATOR PUTS IN AN APPEARANCE,
AND FINALLY LETS US IN.
BUT HE HAS TO GO OVER ALL THE MAIN RULES,
BEFORE HE CAN ACTUALLY LET US BEGIN.

SO I'M NOT ALLOWED TO TALK,
AND I'M NOT ALLOWED TO CHEAT.
AND I'VE BECOME SO BLOODY TERRIFIED,
THAT I CAN HEAR MY THUMPING HEARTBEAT.

SO I FOCUS ALL MY ATTENTION,
ON FILLING IN MY NAME AND THE DATE.
THEN I MAKE THE SIGN OF THE CROSS,
AND HOPE MY SUDDEN FAITH SWITCH ISN'T TOO LATE.

BUT I STILL CAN'T BLOODY START, THOUGH,
AS EACH EXAM PAPER HAS ITS OWN SPECIAL RULES.
SO I READ THEM VERY CAREFULLY,
WHILST FIDDLING WITH MY TOOLS.

AND I'VE BROUGHT SEVERAL ERASER-CAPPED PENCILS,
BUT NO CALCULATOR.
AND AS THIS IS A MATHS EXAM,
I HURRIEDLY SIGNAL FOR THE MODERATOR.

SO I QUICKLY EXPLAIN MY PREDICAMENT,
BUT THE GUY SYMPATHETICALLY SHAKES HIS HEAD.
AND THEN I REALISE THAT MY STUPID BLUNDER
HAS LEFT ME COMPLETELY DONE AND DEAD.

AND I CAN'T ATTEMPT THIS EXAM WITHOUT A CALCULATOR,
NOT LIKE THE OTHER SWATS AND GO-GETTERS.
SO I JUST RESIGN MYSELF TO FAILURE,
AND SCRAWL DOWN "BOLLOCKS!" IN BIG CAPITAL LETTERS!

TEENAGERS

THEY SULK IN THEIR HOODIES,
AND BARELY SPEAK.
JUST THE OCCASIONAL GRUNT
WHEN THEIR INPUT WE SEEK.

AND SPEAKING OF LANGUAGE,
THEY MAKE UP THEIR OWN.
WHICH LEAVES US SCRATCHING OUR HEADS,
AND FEELING ALONE.

AND THEY'RE OFTEN VERY SECRETIVE,
AND IN A BAD MOOD.
HAVE QUESTIONABLE PERSONAL HABITS,
AND SEEM TO PRACTISE BEING RUDE.

THEY ALSO HANG AROUND IN PACKS,
AND ROAM THROUGH THE STREETS.
ATTACHED TO THEIR COLOURFUL HEADPHONES,
EMITTING STRANGE SOUNDING BEATS.

SO THEY'RE UNDERGOING PHYSICAL AND EMOTIONAL CHANGE,
THIS MUCH WE KNOW.
AND THEY SHOW VERY LITTLE INTEREST
IN MAINTAINING THE OVERALL STATUS QUO.

AND THEY ALSO LIKE TAKING RISKS,
AND DON'T SEEM TO CARE.
AND THE LADS GET ALL MACHO,
ABOUT EACH NEW FACIAL HAIR.

NOW, SOME LIKE DOING TRICKS ON THEIR BOARDS OR BIKES,
AND GETTING COVERED IN DIRT.
AND WE CONSTANTLY STRESS AND WORRY,
THAT THEY'RE GOING TO GET HURT.

WHILE OTHERS SPEND THEIR TIME ON PHONES OR LAPTOPS,
COMMUNICATING WITH THEIR FRIENDS.
BUT WE CAN'T WAIT EITHER WAY
UNTIL THEIR ADOLESCENCE FINALLY ENDS.

SO WE DO OUR BEST TO KEEP THEM ON TRACK,
AND GOING TO SCHOOL.
AND THEY DESPISE US FOR OUR EFFORTS,
AND CALL US UNCOOL.

AND THEY THINK THEY KNOW BEST,
AND THEY THINK THEY KNOW IT ALL.
BUT THEY'RE IN FOR A TERRIBLE SHOCK SOON,
AND ONE ALMIGHTY FALL!

GLASSES

I HAVE TO WEAR GLASSES ALL THE TIME,
BECAUSE I'M AS BLIND AS A BAT.
EVEN THOUGH THEY MAKE ME LOOK GOOFY,
AND I SERIOUSLY HATE THAT.

AND I CAN'T EVEN WEAR CONTACT LENSES,
AS I'VE GOT EXTREMELY DRY EYES.
WHICH, GIVEN ALL MY HEALTH PROBLEMS
SHOULDN'T REALLY COME AS A SURPRISE.

AND ALTHOUGH I DESPISE WEARING SPECTACLES,
I HATE BREAKING THEM EVEN MORE.
AND I'M SURE MANY OF YOU CAN SYMPATHISE
ON THAT PARTICULAR SCORE.

SO IT'S A SERIOUSLY STRESSFUL MOMENT,
EVEN BORDERING ON THE TRAUMATIC.
AS IS GETTING USED TO A NEW PAIR,
WHICH, FOR ME, IS NEVER AUTOMATIC.

AND I NEVER KNOW WHEN THEY'RE GOING TO BREAK,
WHICH IS WHY IT'S SUCH A SHOCK.
THEN I HAVE TO PRAY I'M CARRYING MY SPARE PAIR,
WHICH ISN'T AN AUTOMATIC LOCK.

AND IT'S THE SORT OF DAY-RUINING MOMENT
THAT SHOULD BRING A TEAR TO MY EYE.
BUT MY TEAR GLANDS DON'T WORK, OF COURSE,
SO I CAN'T EVEN CRY.

AND I ALSO DISLIKE VISITING THE OPTICIANS, TOO,
BUT I'LL SAVE THAT FOR ANOTHER TIME.
AS THAT'S A SUBJECT WITH PLENTY OF MATERIAL,
THAT'LL EASILY FILL ANOTHER RHYME!

Rough Sex:

Brian was beginning to really feel the effects
after having a week of rough sex.
  He'd taken his new girlfriend camping,
  suffered serious cramping,
and had broken his spare pair of specs.

133

OPTICIANS

I LOATHE HAVING TO GO TO THE OPTICIANS,
FOR ONE VERY SIMPLE FACT.
AS IT MEANS MY MAIN PAIR OF GLASSES,
ARE NO LONGER INTACT.

AND I'LL BE WEARING MY SPARE PAIR, TOO,
THE CHEAP AND NASTY FREE SHIT.
WHICH IS WHY I'LL BE SERIOUSLY PISSED OFF,
AND HISSING A FIT.

AND THE STAFF WON'T CARE THAT I'M DISTRESSED, OF COURSE,
THEY WON'T GIVE A FLYING TOSS.
AS THEY'RE ONLY INTERESTED IN THE GAIN THEY'LL MAKE
FROM MY SIGNIFICANT LOSS.

YOU SEE, THEY ONLY CARE ABOUT MY CASH,
AND GETTING AS MUCH OF IT AS THEY CAN.
SO IT'S JUST ANOTHER INSTANCE OF CORPORATE GREED
SCREWING OVER THE POOR, COMMON MAN.

AND HAVE YOU NOTICED HOW SPECTACLES
NEVER SEEM TO GET ANY FUCKING CHEAPER?
AND I SWEAR THEY KEEP LOOKING FOR NEW WAYS
OF ACTUALLY MAKING THE PRICES STEEPER.

BUT ALL THAT PALES INTO INSIGNIFICANCE, THOUGH,
COMPARED TO THE REAL FUN AND GAMES.
WHEN I HAVE TO GO THROUGH THE CONSIDERABLE STRESS
OF CHOOSING A NEW PAIR OF FRAMES.

AND I ALWAYS STRUGGLE TO FIND ANYTHING SUITABLE,
FROM THE CURRENT STOCK OF STYLES.
WHICH LEADS TO HOURS OF GLOOMY FROWNING,
AND VERY FEW GENUINE SMILES.

AND THIS MAKES ALL THE STAFF MISERABLE, TOO,
BUT I HAVE TO FIND THE PAIR THAT SUITS ME BEST.
AND I'M USUALLY SO EXHAUSTED BY THE END
THAT I NEED TO GO HOME AND HAVE A REST!

IRRITABLE BOWEL SYNDROME

I KNEW A WORK COLLEAGUE WHO SUFFERED WITH THIS,
AND HE WAS ALWAYS POPPING TO THE LOO.
AND THAT WAS LESS TO DO WITH PEEING,
AND MORE TO DO WITH GOING NUMBER TWO.

AND HE REALLY HATED LEAVING HOME, OF COURSE,
WHICH ALWAYS FILLED HIM WITH UTTER DREAD.
UNTIL HE DISCOVERED THAT HIS VICIOUS I.B.S.,
WAS ACTUALLY CAUSED BY HIM EATING FUCKING BREAD!

Messy Secretary:

This is the smelly tale of a poor woman named Jess
who left every toilet she used in a mess.
    She was a secretary from Luton
    and unknowingly allergic to gluten,
which was the cause of her vicious IBS.

MOLE

IT'S NOT A BIRTHMARK OR A BEAUTY SPOT
IT'S JUST A PLAIN, SIMPLE MOLE.
AND BEFORE YOU GET AHEAD OF YOURSELF,
IT'S NOT SITUATED ON MY POLE.

SO IT'S ACTUALLY LOCATED
ON THE LEFT SIDE OF MY FACE.
AND IT'S REALLY RATHER LARGE,
AND TAKES UP SOME CONSIDERABLE SPACE.

BUT IT'S NOT SHAPED LIKE ANYTHING FUN, THOUGH,
NOT LIKE THE BIRTHMARK ON MY BUM.
AND I DID LOOK INTO GETTING IT REMOVED,
BUT THE HIGH COST LEFT ME FEELING QUITE GLUM.

SO I DECIDED TO KEEP MY HARD-EARNED MONEY,
AND NOT GIVE IT TO THOSE LASER-WIELDING CROOKS.
EVEN THOUGH MY MOLE SERIOUSLY DETRACTS
FROM MY ALREADY HIDEOUS LOOKS!

POINTLESS IRONING

WHEN IT COMES TO IRONING MY LAUNDRY,
I DON'T REALLY DO THAT MUCH.
JUST THE ODD THING FOR WORK,
LIKE A CLEAN SHIRT AND SUCH.

AND I CAN'T SEE THE POINT OF IRONING STUFF,
WHICH NO ONE'S GONNA SEE.
SO I JUST ROUGHLY FOLD IT UP,
AND LEAVE IT THE FUCK BE.

AND I MAY OWN A SMALL TRAVEL IRON,
BUT I DON'T OWN AN IRONING BOARD.
I JUST THROW A TOWEL OVER THE COFFEE TABLE,
AND GRAB AN EXTENSION CORD.

AND LIFE'S FAR TOO BLOODY SHORT,
TO WASTE TIME IRONING POINTLESS SHIT.
SO I'D RATHER STUFF IT IN A DRAWER,
AND JUST FORGET ABOUT IT.

AND I DON'T IRON MY FRIGGING T-SHIRTS,
OR MY SOCKS AND MY PANTS.
HELL, I'D RATHER GOUGE MY EYES OUT,
WITH A LONG JOUSTING LANCE.

AND THE SAME GOES FOR MY JEANS,
AND ALL THE TOWELS I WASH, TOO.
BECAUSE I HATE POINTLESS IRONING,
AND I'VE GOT BETTER THINGS TO DO!

QUEUE ETIQUETTE

THIS IS A BRITISH-BORN PHENOMENON,
THAT'S SADLY ON THE DECLINE.
AS MORE AND MORE BRITS CAN'T BE BOTHERED
TO FORM AN ORDERLY LINE.

AND WE USED TO QUEUE VERY NEATLY,
AND HAVE A NEIGHBOURLY GRUMBLE.
BUT NOW OUR QUEUES ARE STARTING TO RESEMBLE
SOMETHING OUT OF A WRESTLING ROYAL RUMBLE.

NOW, THE ETIQUETTE OF QUEUEING
ACTUALLY DATES BACK TO THE SECOND WORLD WAR.
WHEN WE HAD TO QUEUE UP FOR OUR RATIONS
AND OUR PATIENCE WASN'T SO POOR.

AND THE RULES WERE VERY SIMPLE,
AND REVOLVED AROUND YOU KNOWING YOUR PLACE.
AND BEING PREPARED AT ANY SECOND
TO SHUFFLE INTO A SUDDEN APPEARING SPACE.

BUT THE RULES AREN'T BEING OBEYED NOW,
WHICH HAS BECOME A MAJOR CONCERN.
AS MORE AND MORE PEOPLE CAN'T BE ARSED
TO WAIT THEIR FUCKING TURN.

AND THEY'RE ALWAYS IN SUCH A HURRY,
AND NEEDING TO SUDDENLY DASH.
WHICH IS WHY IT'S NO SURPRISE
THAT SOME PEOPLE'S TEMPERS CLASH.

AND YOU'VE HEARD OF ROAD RAGE, OF COURSE,
BUT QUEUE RAGE ALSO EXISTS.
AS IT DOESN'T TAKE ALL THAT MUCH
FOR PEOPLE TO START USING THEIR FISTS.

AND IT'S USUALLY CAUSED BY SOME BARGING BULLY,
BECAUSE THEY DON'T HAVE MUCH TIME.
WHICH IS NOT ONLY SOCIALLY UNACCEPTABLE,
BUT ALSO A SERIOUS ETIQUETTE CRIME.

AND I'M NOT A BIG FAN OF QUEUEING MYSELF,
AND I'D GUESS NEITHER ARE YOU.
BUT I STILL GET A THRILL WHEN THE QUEUE THAT I'M IN
BEATS ANOTHER QUEUE!

OBVIOUS STATEMENTS

PEOPLE WHO STATE THE FUCKING OBVIOUS,
DRIVE ME COMPLETELY INSANE.
AND I HAVE TO FIGHT NOT TO STRANGLE THEM,
OR INFLICT MAXIMUM PAIN.

AND I CAN SEE THAT IT'S RAINING,
OR THE TIME IS CURRENTLY MIDDAY.
SO THEY SHOULD EITHER SHUT THE FUCK UP,
OR FIND SOMETHING MORE USEFUL TO SAY.

AND IT'S ACTUALLY GOLF COMMENTATORS ON TV,
WHO ARE GUILTY OF THIS THE MOST.
AS TELLING ME STUFF THAT I CAN ALREADY SEE,
MAKES THEM A REALLY SHIT HOST.

AND THEY TROT OUT THE SAME FUCKING GUFF,
YEAR AFTER SODDING YEAR.
WHICH IS WHY THEY DRIVE ME BLOODY LOOPY,
AND HAVE BECOME SO PAINFUL TO HEAR.

AND I KNOW THEIR JOBS ARE VERY TRICKY,
AS THEY HAVE TO FILL HUGE AMOUNTS OF TIME.
BUT I STILL WANT THEM TO STOP GIVING ME INFO,
THAT'S ALREADY WELL PAST ITS PRIME.

AND THEY SHOULD DO SOME BETTER RESEARCH,
AND COME UP WITH SOMETHING THAT'S FRESH.
SO I'M NOT LEFT SCREAMING AT THE TELEVISION,
AND WANTING TO RIP OFF MY OWN FLESH!

Irish Golfer:

There was an abysmal Irish golfer called Ferdy
who was desperate to score his first birdie.
　　He kept taking lessons with the pro
　　who gladly took all his dough
and then advised him to take up the hurdy-gurdy.

HYPER-CHEERFUL PEOPLE

PEOPLE WHO ARE RELENTLESSLY HYPER-CHEERFUL,
DRIVE ME EVEN MORE FUCKING INSANE.
IT'S LIKE BEING AROUND THE ENERGIZER BUNNY,
WHEN IT'S SMOKING CRACK COCAINE.

AND THEY'RE ALWAYS SO FUCKING POSITIVE,
AND CONSTANTLY BOUNCING AROUND.
WHICH IS WHY I WANT TO KEEP PUNCHING THEM,
UNTIL THEY'RE HUGGING THE GROUND.

BUT IT'S ACTUALLY THE WAY THAT THEY TALK,
THAT I FIND THE MOST DISTRACTING.
AND IF YOU'VE EVER MET ONE OF THESE PEOPLE,
THEN YOU KNOW I'M NOT OVERREACTING.

AND THEY ALWAYS SOUND SO BLOODY EAGER,
AND SEEM TO BE SO SUPER-PUMPED.
SO IT'S A MIRACLE THEY MAKE IT THROUGH THE DAY,
WITHOUT BEING SERIOUSLY THUMPED.

AND THESE PEOPLE AREN'T ACTING, OF COURSE,
OR DELIBERATELY TRYING TO BE FRUSTRATING.
AS THEY WERE BORN WITH THEIR ETERNAL OPTIMISM,
AND ARE THEREFORE JUST NATURALLY GRATING.

AND THEY EVEN REMAIN TOTALLY OPTIMISTIC,
IN SITUATIONS OF GENUINE GLOOM.
WHICH IS WHEN MY NERVES FINALLY FRAY,
AND I'M FORCED TO LEAVE THE FUCKING ROOM!

SHOPPING

THERE ARE TWO TYPES OF SHOPPING,
FUN AND REQUIRED.
AND OF THOSE TWO,
ONLY ONE IS DESIRED.

SO LET'S BEGIN WITH THE REQUIRED OPTION,
TO GET IT OUT OF THE WAY.
WHERE WE TRUDGE TO THE SUPERMARKET,
FIND OUR GROCERIES, GRAB, QUEUE AND PAY.

AND NOW THAT WE'VE DEALT WITH THE DULL STUFF,
LET'S MOVE ON TO THE GOLD.
AS SHOPPING FOR THE FUN STUFF,
NEVER GETS OLD.

BUT THE QUESTION NOW, THOUGH,
IS WHERE DO WE START?
AS THERE ARE SO MANY GREAT CHOICES,
WHICH BRING JOY TO THE HEART.

SO LET'S BEGIN WITH SOME CLOTHES AND ACCESSORIES,
AND EVEN A NICE PAIR OF SHOES.
MAYBE SOME *HUGO BOSS* OR *VERSACE*,
AND THEN SOME *MANOLO BLAHNIK'S* OR *JIMMY CHOO'S*.

BUT MOST OF US CAN'T AFFORD THOSE NAMES,
AS WE JUST DON'T HAVE THE BUCKS.
SO WE HAVE TO MAKE DO WITH SOME KNOCKED-OFF *GUCCI*,
SOLD FROM THE BACKS OF DUBIOUS TRUCKS.

NOW, LET'S MOVE ON FROM THE STUFF WE WEAR,
TO ALL THE TECHNOLOGY AND GADGETS.
WHICH ARE SHINY, EXCITING TO PLAY WITH,
AND CREATE MANY, MANY BAD HABITS.

SOME OF THEM CAN COST A FORTUNE, THOUGH,
AND EVEN LET YOU PLACE BETS.
WHICH EXPLAINS WHY I'M ALMOST BANKRUPT,
AND STILL SWIFTLY RUNNING UP DEBTS.

SO WE'LL QUICKLY FINISH WITH MY FUN FAVOURITES,
WHICH ARE OF COURSE MUSIC AND FILMS.
AND THERE ARE LITERALLY MILLIONS TO CHOOSE FROM,
THAT COVER ALL GENRES AND REALMS.

AND I LOVE ROCK AND POP MUSIC,
AND URBAN, INDIE AND TRANCE.
ALONG WITH GREAT COMEDIES AND ACTION THRILLERS,
AND THE ODD MURDER MYSTERY FROM FRANCE!

ARGUMENTS

AN ARGUMENT CAN BE STARTED,
BY THE SMALLEST OR SIMPLEST THING.
SUCH AS, NOT MAKING A PHONE CALL,
WHEN WE SAID WE'D ACTUALLY RING.

AND THEN THINGS JUST SNOWBALL FROM THERE,
AND SOON WE'RE LOSING CONTROL.
WHICH IS WHEN WE BEGIN THROWING THINGS,
AND REACH FOR ANOTHER BOWL.

BUT NOT ALL ARGUMENTS GO THERMONUCLEAR, THOUGH,
AND CAUSE US JUST TO SNAP.
BECAUSE THERE'RE THINGS WE ARGUE ABOUT EVERY DAY,
LIKE ALL THE NORMAL CRAP.

SO STUFF LIKE, ARGUING ABOUT CONTROL OF THE REMOTE,
AND WHAT WE WANT TO WATCH.
AND WHETHER TO HAVE A GLASS OF RED WINE,
OR JUST TO POUR ANOTHER SCOTCH.

AND WE ALSO ARGUE IN MEETINGS AT WORK,
WHICH THEN SPILLS OVER TO LUNCH.
AND ALL BECAUSE OUR BOSS IS PISSED,
THAT WE PLAYED A RISKY HUNCH.

THEN WE ARGUE ABOUT OUR POLITICS,
AND HOW WE'RE GOING TO VOTE.
IGNORING THE AGE-OLD FACT, OF COURSE,
THAT THERE'RE NO POLITICAL RUNNERS WORTHY OF NOTE.

SO LATER WE ARGUE ABOUT GOING OUT TO DINNER,
AND WHAT WE'RE GOING TO WEAR.
AND THEN WE'RE READY IN LESS THAN TEN MINUTES,
WHICH IS AN EVENT THAT'S TERRIBLY RARE.

THEN WE ARGUE ABOUT WHO'S DRIVING,
AND THE BEST ROUTE THAT WE SHOULD TAKE.
AND WHEN WE GET TO THE RESTAURANT,
WE'LL ARGUE OVER HAVING THE CHICKEN OR THE STEAK.

WE ALSO ARGUE ABOUT THE SEX OF OUR FIRST CHILD,
AND POSSIBLE BABY NAMES.
AND ON THEIR FIRST TRIP TO THE FAIRGROUND,
WE'LL ARGUE OVER THEM GOING ON RIDES OR GAMES.

WE ALSO ARGUE ABOUT WHEN EXACTLY THEY'LL BE BORN,
AND HOW TO CELEBRATE.
THEN WE GO BACK TO ARGUING ABOUT NURSERY COLOURS,
AND HOW TO DECORATE.

AND WE EVEN ARGUE WHEN WE GO TO THE MOVIES,
ABOUT WHAT WE WANT TO SEE.
IF WE SHOULD CHECK OUT ANOTHER ACTION FILM,
OR WATCH A COMEDY.

AND AN ARGUMENT CAN BE FINISHED,
JUST AS QUICKLY AS IT BEGAN.
SIMPLY BY PROFUSELY APOLOGISING,
AND BEING THE BIGGER MAN!

Bickering Couple:

A constantly bickering couple said enough is enough
and decided to divide up their stuff.
    She kept anything with style,
    he got the rest of the pile,
and when he complained she said it was tough.

"I'M BACK!"

PEOPLE WHO LOUDLY ANNOUNCE, *"I'M BACK!"*
AS SOON AS THEY GET HOME.
DRIVE ME TOTALLY FUCKING CRAZY,
AND CAUSE MY MOUTH TO FOAM.

AND I'VE GOT TWO EYES AND EARS,
WHICH MEANS I CAN HEAR AND SEE.
SO SHUT THE FUCK UP FOR CHRIST'S SAKE,
AND JUST LEAVE ME BE!

QUEUEING

LET'S BEGIN WITH QUEUEING IN TRAFFIC,
WHICH IS A POINTLESS WASTE OF FUEL.
THEN WE HAVE TO QUEUE TO BUY MORE PETROL,
WHICH SEEMS IRONIC AND FUCKING CRUEL.

WE ALSO HAVE TO QUEUE TO BUY OUR GROCERIES,
AND AGAIN WHEN WE LEAVE IN THE CAR.
AND WE MIGHT HAVE TO QUEUE IN SOME ROADWORKS, TOO,
UNLESS DRIVING HOME ISN'T VERY FAR.

SO WE HAVE TO QUEUE FOR OUR MORNING COFFEE,
AND THEN AGAIN AT LUNCH.
AND WE HAVE TO QUEUE THROUGHOUT THE DAY,
TO BUY THE SNACKS ON WHICH WE MUNCH.

AND SOMETIMES WE HAVE TO QUEUE FOR THE TOILET,
WHEN WE DESPERATELY NEED TO GO.
AND THEN WE FIND THERE'S NO TOILET PAPER,
WHICH CAUSES OUR TOP TO BLOW.

WE ALSO HAVE TO QUEUE TO SEE OUR DOCTOR,
AND THEN AGAIN TO GET OUR PILLS.
AND WE EVEN HAVE TO QUEUE AT THE POST OFFICE,
TO PAY OUR WRETCHED BILLS.

AND WE HAVE TO QUEUE TO PAY MONEY INTO THE BANK,
AND THEN AGAIN TO GET IT OUT.
AND BEFORE THAT, WE HAD TO QUEUE IN THE CAR PARK,
WHICH MADE US WANT TO SHOUT.

WE ALSO HAVE TO QUEUE TO GET INTO THE CINEMA,
AND AFTERWARDS FOR SOME FAST FOOD.
THEN WE GO BACK TO QUEUEING IN THE PHARMACY,
FOR SOMETHING TO LIGHTEN OUR MOOD.

AND WE ALWAYS HAVE TO QUEUE IN HOSPITALS,
WHICH DRIVES US RIDICULOUSLY MAD.
BUT IT'S WHEN WE'RE QUEUEING FOR OUR DRY-CLEANING
THAT WE KNOW THAT THINGS ARE BAD.

WE ALSO HAVE TO QUEUE TO PLACE A BET,
AND BEFORE THE HORSES GET TO THE TRACK.
AND THEN OUR CHOSEN NAG FAILS TO LEAVE THE STALLS,
WHICH ALSO CAUSES US TO CRACK.

SO WE SHOULD REMEMBER AS WE GO THROUGH LIFE
THAT WE'LL ALWAYS ENCOUNTER QUEUES.
BUT IF WE CAN CONTROL OUR LEVELS OF FRUSTRATION,
THEN WE MIGHT JUST AVOID THOSE QUEUEING BLUES!

DIETING

DIETING WITHOUT SOME FORM OF EXERCISE
IS A COMPLETE WASTE OF TIME.
BUT IF YOU'RE UP FOR THE DUAL CHALLENGE,
THEN JUST KEEP READING THIS RHYME.

AND COMBINING THE TWO IS FAIRLY EASY,
WHEN YOU KNOW WHAT TO DO.
AS YOU JUST NEED TO DRAW UP A SENSIBLE PLAN,
AND THEN OBVIOUSLY STICK TO IT, TOO.

SO START BY EATING PLENTY OF FRESH FRUIT AND VEGGIES,
AND A DECENT AMOUNT OF RICE.
AND I KNOW THAT SOUNDS TERRIBLY BLAND,
BUT YOU CAN STILL MAKE IT TASTE FAIRLY NICE.

AND THEN YOU CAN THROW IN SOME LEAN CHICKEN,
OR A NICE PIECE OF FISH.
AS YOU DON'T NEED TO BE A TALENTED CHEF,
TO CREATE AN APPETISING DISH.

AND AS FOR THE EXERCISE PART,
JUST GO FOR A DECENT DAILY WALK.
BUT DON'T BECOME ONE OF THOSE PEOPLE, THOUGH,
WHO ARE ALL FUCKING TALK.

AND IF YOU DON'T FANCY WALKING,
THEN FIND SOMETHING ELSE YOU'LL LIKE.
AS, WHEN IT'S TOO WET TO GO OUT FOR A WALK,
I JUMP ON MY EXERCISE BIKE.

YOU'LL ALSO NEED TO CUT DOWN THE SNACKS AND BREAD,
AND OTHER BAKED GOODS.
AND THEN THERE ARE THE CAKES AND ICE-CREAM,
AND OTHER AFTER-MEAL PUDS.

BUT YOU'LL SOON NOTICE THE DIFFERENCE, THOUGH,
WITH A LITTLE WILLPOWER.
SO JUST BLOODY GET ON WITH IT,
AND DON'T LOOK SO FUCKING SOUR!

TURNING THIRTY

TURNING THIRTY IS A SIGNAL
THAT THINGS ARE GOING TO CHANGE.
BUT THE INITIAL DIFFERENCES ARE SO SLIGHT,
THAT THEY DON'T APPEAR STRANGE.

AND IT BEGINS WITH AVOIDING CERTAIN PLACES
WHERE THERE'S TOO MUCH NOISE.
WHICH MEANS, LESS ROWDY NIGHTS OUT
WITH THE OTHER GIRLS AND BOYS.

BUT OUR FRIENDS ARE SLOWING DOWN, TOO,
SO THIS DOESN'T ACTUALLY MATTER.
AND WE'RE SOON CONGREGATING IN QUIETER PUBS,
WHERE WE CAN HEAR OURSELVES NATTER.

AND THEN COMES THE URGE TO PAIR UP,
AND SETTLE DOWN WITH A MATE.
BUT AS EVERYONE ELSE IS DOING IT,
WE DON'T REALISE OUR LIFE'S BECOMING SEDATE.

SO NEXT COMES THE SUBJECT OF MONEY,
WHICH GETS A MORE SERIOUS MENTION.
LIKE, SAVING FOR MUCH NICER HOLIDAYS,
AND EVEN STARTING A PENSION.

AND THEN THERE'S TALK OF HAVING KIDS,
AND BUYING OUR VERY OWN HOUSE.
AND QUITE SOON OUR LIFE'S LESS ABOUT US,
AND MUCH MORE ABOUT OUR SPOUSE.

SO OUR NIGHTS OUT ALSO CONTINUE TO DRY UP,
AS OUR BODIES CAN'T TAKE THE ABUSE.
AND WE GET MUCH BETTER AT LYING, TOO,
AND THINKING UP AN EXCUSE.

AND WE ALSO START GOING TO BED A LOT EARLIER,
AS WE NEED THE EXTRA REST.
PLUS, WE'RE HAVING LESS AND LESS SEX,
AS WE'RE NO LONGER AT OUR PHYSICAL BEST.

AND THEN BEFORE WE ACTUALLY REALISE IT,
WE'VE BECOME A BORING OLD FART.
AS WE'RE JUST GOING THROUGH THE MOTIONS,
AND PLAYING OUR TEDIOUS PART!

STRESS

I NEVER REALISED THAT I WAS STRESSED,
NOT UNTIL I SAW THE WEIRD RASH ON MY ARM.
BUT THE EARLY WARNING SIGNS WERE ALWAYS THERE,
AND SHOULD HAVE RAISED AN ALARM.

AND I'M TALKING ABOUT THE INVISIBLE STUFF, OF COURSE,
ALL THE THINGS I COULDN'T SEE.
LIKE, FEELING ANXIOUS OR OVERWHELMED,
OR HAVING AN INCREASED URGE TO PEE.

AND IF I'D SPOTTED THE CLUES IN TIME,
THEN I COULD'VE HEADED IT OFF AT THE JUNCTION.
WHICH WOULD'VE CERTAINLY BEEN MORE PREFERABLE,
THAN ME GETTING ERECTILE DYSFUNCTION.

BUT IT DID GIVE ME A CONSIDERABLE BREAK, THOUGH,
FROM ALL THE CHAFFING AND BLISTERS.
AS I SUDDENLY HAD VERY LITTLE USE
FOR AUNTY PALM AND HER FIVE WIGGLY SISTERS.

SO I THINK THAT'S WHAT THEY CALL IRONY,
ASSUMING I'M ACTUALLY TELLING THE TRUTH.
AND THIS COULD ALL BE LIES, OF COURSE,
OR ME JUST TAKING AN OPPORTUNITY TO BE UNCOUTH.

SO LET'S MOVE ON TO MY SLEW OF STOMACH PROBLEMS NEXT,
WHICH WERE FAR TOO NUMEROUS TO NAME.
AND ALTHOUGH THEY'VE CONSIDERABLY SUBSIDED NOW,
THINGS STILL DON'T FEEL QUITE THE SAME.

AND I'VE NO IDEA WHAT BROUGHT ON MY STRESS,
I JUST DON'T HAVE THE FIRST CLUE.
AS IT SEEMED TO MATERIALISE VERY SLOWLY,
AND THEN JUMP RIGHT OUT OF THE BLUE.

BUT I KNOW IT'S TWISTED MY GUTS INTO A KNOT,
AND IS SERIOUSLY MESSING WITH MY HEAD.
AND IF I DON'T GET A HANDLE ON IT SOON,
THEN I'LL STRUGGLE TO GET MY ARSE OUT OF BED!

NARCOLEPSY

NOW, I'M NOT COMPLETELY WITHOUT FEELING,
AND I'M NOT BLINDLY UNAWARE.
BUT THIS SUBJECT'S TOO HUMOROUS TO PASS UP,
SO I JUST DON'T FUCKING CARE.

AND IT'S NOT JUST PEOPLE WHO GET THIS, YOU SEE,
IT'S ALSO ANIMALS, TOO.
AND WHAT COULD BE FUNNIER THAN A DOG DOZING OFF,
WHILE IT'S DOING A MASSIVE POO.

AND BEFORE YOU WRITE ME OFF AS SOME SICKO,
WHO ENJOYS WATCHING CANINES TAKING A DUMP.
AT LEAST TAKE A LOOK FOR YOURSELF,
AS I'M HARDLY A PERVERTED CHUMP.

AND I KNOW THAT NARCOLEPSY'S A BRAIN DISORDER,
WHICH IS EXTREMELY RARE.
BUT WHO DOESN'T LOVE A NARCOLEPTIC KITTEN,
WHEN IT'S FALLING OFF OF A CHAIR.

SO ARE WE BACK ON SOLID GROUND YET,
OR DO YOU STILL THINK I'M BEING CRUEL?
AS THIS IS ONE TERRIFIC TOPIC,
WITH A LOT MORE HILARIOUS FUEL.

AND I'M BEING REALLY SERIOUS ABOUT THIS,
AS IT'S AN ABUNDANCE OF GIGGLING RICHES.
SO JUST GOOGLE *"NARCOLEPTIC ANIMALS"*,
AND IT'LL HAVE YOU IN ABSOLUTE STITCHES.

AND THE CLIPS AREN'T JUST OF CATS AND DOGS, OF COURSE,
AS THERE ARE HORSES AS WELL.
BUT LAUGHING WHEN THEY FINALLY COLLAPSE
WILL GENERATE US A SPECIAL PLACE IN HELL.

AND THERE ARE LOTS OF GOATS TO SEE, ALSO,
AND EVEN AN ADORABLE, FAINTING FAWN.
AS WELL AS TONS OF CUTE PUPPIES AND KITTENS,
WHICH HAVE JUST RECENTLY BEEN BORN.

SO ARE YOU DOING BETTER WITH THIS NOW,
OR ARE YOU STILL PITCHING A FIT?
AND I DON'T KNOW ABOUT YOU,
BUT I CAN'T GET ENOUGH OF THIS AMUSING SHIT.

AND IF YOU REALLY WANT TO MOVE ON TO PEOPLE,
THERE'S A BOY BOWLING OR A SWEET BABY GIRL.
BUT MY MOST FAVOURITE CLIP OF ALL
IS THAT OF A CUTE, NARCOLEPTIC SQUIRREL!

COLD SORE

YOU CAN TRUST ME WHEN I TELL YOU,
THAT YOU NEVER WANT TO GET ONE OF THESE.
A NASTY, FLUID-FILLED BLISTER,
WHOSE CLINICAL NAME BEGINS WITH HERPES.

AND THE *HERPES SIMPLEX VIRUS*,
WHICH IS ALSO KNOWN AS *HSV-1*.
IS VERY UNPLEASANT TO LOOK AT,
AND ABSOLUTELY NO SODDING FUN.

AND IT SNEAKILY FORMS UNSEEN,
WITH A TINGLING, ITCHING OR BURNING SENSATION.
THEN IT LASTS FOR 7 TO 20 DAYS,
WHICH IS LONGER THAN MY LAST FUCKING VACATION.

AND THE VIRUS CAN LIE DORMANT WITHIN YOU,
UNTIL IT FINALLY GETS TRIGGERED.
SO YOU DON'T KNOW YOU'VE GOT IT,
UNTIL YOUR MOUTH BECOMES HORRIBLY DISFIGURED.

AND THE TRIGGERS ARE USUALLY QUITE SIMPLE,
LIKE A SMALL FACIAL INJURY OR FATIGUE.
THEN YOU'RE LEFT HATING THE SIGHT OF YOUR OWN FACE,
AND FEELING OUT OF YOUR LEAGUE.

AND THE SORE CAN BE TREATED BY AN ANTIVIRAL CREAM,
IF YOU CATCH IT EARLY ENOUGH.
BUT ONCE THE BLISTER'S STARTED FORMING,
YOU'RE WASTING YOUR CASH BUYING THE STUFF.

SO I PERSONALLY CAUGHT THE VIRUS,
FROM SIMPLY BEING KISSED.
AND I DIDN'T SPOT THE GIRL'S COLD SORE,
BECAUSE I WAS SERIOUSLY PISSED.

SO NOW I'M STUCK WITH THEM FOR LIFE,
AND CAN'T EVEN HIDE THEM WITH MY BEARD.
WHICH IS WHY I ALWAYS WEAR A BALACLAVA,
UNTIL THEY'VE ACTUALLY CLEARED!

WRONG NUMBERS

THIS IS SOMETHING ELSE THAT DRIVES ME CRAZY,
WHICH IS WHY I'M HAVING A MOAN.
BECAUSE I'M STILL GETTING WRONG NUMBER CALLS,
TO MY MOBILE BLOODY PHONE.

AND THE REASON I'M SO ANGRY ABOUT THIS,
AND JUST SO INCREDIBLY PISSED.
IS BECAUSE THE CALLER'S TYPED THE NUMBER INCORRECTLY
INTO THEIR CONTACTS LIST.

AND THEN THEY JUST KEEP CALLING AND CALLING,
EXPECTING THE NUMBER TO HAVE MAGICALLY CHANGED.
SO I POINT OUT HOW FUCKING RETARDED THEY ARE,
WHILST BECOMING MENTALLY DERANGED.

AND, YEAH, I KNOW, I KNOW,
THAT I SHOULDN'T USE THE R-WORD.
BUT GETTING WRONG CALLS FROM OTHER CELL PHONES
IS JUST SO BLOODY ABSURD.

SO THE NEXT TIME YOU ENTER A NEW CONTACT,
PLEASE, MAKE SURE THE NUMBER IS CORRECT.
THAT WAY YOU WON'T CALL THE WRONG PERSON,
AND GET A LOAD OF VERBAL DISRESPECT.

AND WRONG NUMBER CALLS REALLY ARE UNNECESSARY,
IN THIS TECHNOLOGICAL DAY AND AGE.
WHICH IS WHY I GET SO BLOODY UPSET,
AND THEN DESCEND INTO UNCONTROLLABLE RAGE!

Wrong Number:

There once was an irate dance instructor named Paul
who kept receiving the same wrong number call.
It was seriously screwing with his slumber,
interrupting him practising his rhumba,
and messing with his toilet time worst of all.

NUISANCE CALLS

I'VE ALREADY MOANED ABOUT WRONG NUMBERS,
SO I THOUGHT I'D COVER THESE AS WELL.
AS EACH NUISANCE CALL I GET
IS LIKE BEING SENT TO A FRESH PLACE IN HELL.

AND I KNOW WHAT YOU'RE THINKING NOW,
BUT AREN'T THEY THE SAME FUCKING THING?
BUT NUISANCE CALLS ARE VERY DIFFERENT,
AND LEAVE A FAR MORE PAINFUL STING.

AND THEY ALWAYS CATCH ME, OF COURSE,
AT THE WORST POSSIBLE TIME.
WHICH IS MY REAL MOTIVATION
FOR PENNING THIS GROUCHY RHYME.

AND I'LL BE GETTING READY TO GO OUT,
OR I'LL HAVE JUST GOTTEN HOME FROM WORK.
BUT IT'S WHEN I'M SITTING DOWN TO EAT,
THAT THESE CALLS REALLY DRIVE ME BERSERK.

AND THEY ALL WANT THE SAME THING, OF COURSE,
THEY WANT MY FUCKING MONEY.
WHICH IS WHY THEY'RE WORSE THAN WRONG NUMBERS,
AND NEVER REMOTELY FUNNY.

AND EVEN MY BANK HAS STARTED COLD-CALLING ME,
TO GET MORE OF MY BLOODY CASH.
AND THEY'VE ALREADY GOT ALL MY DOSH,
NOT THAT THAT STOPS THEM FROM GIVING IT A BASH.

AND I ALSO HATE THAT THESE ARSEHOLES CALL ME
WHEN I'M WATCHING THE BLOODY GAME.
AND THAT THEY RUB FURTHER SALT INTO THE WOUND,
BY USING THE SHORTENED VERSION OF MY NAME.

AND THEN THERE'RE ALL THE DODGY SCAMMERS,
AND ALL THE LYING, BAREFACED CHEATS.
WHICH IS WHY I CHANGE MY MOBILE NUMBER MORE OFTEN
THAN I CHANGE MY SODDING SHEETS!

SUPERMARKET SHUFFLE

FINDING THAT CERTAIN PRODUCTS HAVE BEEN MOVED,
ALWAYS CAUSES A SERIOUS KAFUFFLE.
WHICH IS WHY I HATE BEING A VICTIM
OF THE SUPERMARKET SHUFFLE.

AND I DON'T MEAN THE PREMIUM ITEMS,
WHICH ARE ALWAYS CHANGING SITUATIONAL GEARS.
I'M REFERRING TO THE GENUINE, BASIC STAPLES,
WHICH HAVE BEEN IN THE SAME PLACE FOR YEARS.

AND I SWEAR MY STORE MOVES PRODUCTS AROUND,
JUST TO WATCH ME FUCKING CRY.
AS THEY KNOW I SHOP BY SPECIFIC SHELF LOCATIONS,
BASED ON THE THINGS I WANT TO BUY.

AND THEN FINDING SOMETHING'S BEEN MOVED,
ALWAYS SENDS ME INTO A RAGE.
AS FIGURING OUT ITS NEW LOCATION,
IS ALWAYS DIFFICULT TO GAUGE.

AND THEY RECENTLY MOVED THE VINEGAR I LIKE,
WHICH REALLY FREAKED ME OUT.
AS IT HAD BEEN IN THE SAME PLACE FOR 20 YEARS
OR ROUGHLY THERE ABOUT.

AND IT USED TO BE IN THE AISLE WITH THE COOKING OIL,
RIGHT NEXT TO ALL THE SALT.
BUT IT NOT BEING THERE A FEW WEEKS AGO
SOON BROUGHT MY SHOPPING TO A HALT.

AND IT TOOK ME AT LEAST TEN BLOODY MINUTES,
TO FIND ITS NEW RESTING PLACE.
WHICH HAD ME SWEARING UNDER MY BREATH,
AND GOING VERY RED IN THE FACE.

AND WHEN I SAY IT TOOK TEN MINUTES,
I'M NOT JOKING OR PULLING YOUR LEGS.
AS THEY'D MOVED IT HALFWAY ACROSS THE STORE,
AND STUCK IT NEXT TO THE SODDING EGGS!

FLOATERS

THERE REALLY IS NOTHING WORSE
WHEN I'M DROPPING THE KIDS OFF AT THE POOL.
THAN FINDING SOMEONE'S LEFT BEHIND
A LUMP OF THEIR STINKY, FLOATING STOOL.

AND IT'S USUALLY PARTIALLY DISSOLVED,
AND LOOKS SERIOUSLY NASTY.
AND IT ALWAYS HAPPENS AT WORK,
AND PUTS ME OFF MY LUNCHTIME PASTY.

AND I REALLY DON'T UNDERSTAND
WHY PEOPLE CAN'T JUST FUCKING CHECK.
THAT THEY'RE NOT LEAVING SOMETHING BEHIND,
NOT EVEN THE SLIGHTEST SPECK.

AND THE SAME THING MUST HAPPEN TO THEM,
AND I CAN'T IMAGINE THEY ENJOY IT.
NOT UNLESS THEY ACTUALLY GET THEIR JOLLIES
FROM STARING AT OTHER PEOPLES' SHIT.

AND I DON'T THINK I'M ASKING FOR TOO MUCH,
JUST TO GIVE THE BOG AN EXTRA FLUSH.
SO I'M NOT CONFRONTED WITH A BOWL,
THAT'S FILLED WITH ROTTING BROWN MUSH.

AND I COULD GET ONE OF THOSE AUTOMATIC FLUSHERS,
LIKE THAT GUY ON *ALLY McBEAL*.
AS I'M GETTING EXTREMELY SICK AND TIRED
OF SEEING SOME OTHER BLOKE'S PARTLY DIGESTED MEAL!

Mafia Don:

There once was a feared Chicago mafia don
whose nickname was "Bone Crusher" Ron.
    Now, despite being a gangster,
    he was a bit of a prankster,
and often used cellophane to cover the john.

(I'm pretty sure that in the U.S. *john* is used as a slang term for toilet. However, if I'm wrong about this, then it means that this limerick is of no fucking use whatsoever.)

FEARS

THIS RHYME ISN'T GOING TO BE ABOUT PHOBIAS,
OR THE THINGS THAT REDUCE US TO TEARS.
IT'S ABOUT THE STUFF THAT SCARES US SHITLESS,
OUR DEEPEST, DARKEST FEARS.

AND IT'S ALSO GOING TO BE SEXIST,
BECAUSE IT'S ONLY ABOUT GUYS.
BUT THEN, GIVEN I'M A BLOKE,
THAT'S HARDLY A SURPRISE.

SO I'M NOT QUALIFIED TO COMMENT ON WOMEN,
WHICH IS WHY I'M STEERING WELL CLEAR.
AND THAT ALSO BRINGS ME AROUND NICELY,
TO DISCUSSING OUR FIRST FEAR.

AND ALL MEN ARE AFRAID OF WOMEN,
AND THAT'S A CAST IRON FACT.
BUT WE ALL HIDE IT REALLY WELL, THOUGH,
AND HARDLY EVER SHOW IT OR REACT.

AND ANY GUY THAT SAYS DIFFERENT
IS JUST A FLAT OUT LIAR.
BECAUSE, AS SOON AS ANY WOMAN ASKS OUR ADVICE
WE ALL START TO PERSPIRE.

SO LET'S MOVE ON TO OUR NEXT FEAR, THEN,
WHICH WE ALSO HIDE REALLY DEEP.
AS WE'RE ALL TERRIBLY AFRAID
OF BEING MURDERED IN OUR SLEEP.

AND AS AWFUL AS ALL THAT SEEMS,
IT'S STILL NOT OUR MOST FEARFUL NUMBER ONE.
AND NEITHER'S WATCHING PENALTY SHOOTOUTS,
OR WORRYING WE'LL NEVER HAVE A SON.

SO OUR WORST FEAR IS ACTUALLY CASTRATION,
AS NO GUY WANTS TO LOSE HIS PRECIOUS WAND.
NOT WHEN HE'S SPENT SO MUCH TIME PLAYING WITH IT,
AND FORMING AN INSEPARABLE BOND!

BIG WORDS

PEOPLE THAT DELIBERATELY USE BIG WORDS
REALLY GET ON MY TITS.
THOUGH, I TYPICALLY FIND THAT IT'S WRITERS
WHO'RE THE MAIN CULPRITS.

AND I'M SURE THEY THINK THEY'RE BEING CLEVER,
BY USING UNNECESSARILY OBSCURE WORDS.
BUT I'M HERE TO TELL THEM ALL STRAIGHT,
THAT THEY'RE JUST BEING MAJOR TURDS.

SO I FIND THERE'S REALLY NOTHING WORSE,
WHEN I'M READING A GREAT PIECE OF FICTION.
TO COME ACROSS A STRANGE WORD,
THAT'S NOT IN MY OWN DICTION.

AND I'M NOT EVEN SMART ENOUGH TO KNOW,
IF MY USE OF THAT LAST WORD IS CORRECT.
BUT THEN, I'M TRYING TO MAKE YOU LAUGH,
NOT IMPRESS YOU WITH MY INTELLECT.

AND I BLAME *M.S. WORD*, OF COURSE,
WITH ITS HANDY SYNONYM FEATURE.
AS YOU CAN JUST HIGHLIGHT THE WORD *MONSTER*,
AND QUICKLY CHANGE IT TO *CREATURE*.

AND IF THAT DOESN'T WORK,
THEN THERE'S THE BUILT-IN THESAURUS.
AS IT ALLOWS YOU TO FIND ALL THE DIFFERENT WORDS,
WHICH ACTUALLY MEAN *CHORUS*.

AND NOW I'M BEING SILLY, OF COURSE,
BUT I THINK I'VE MADE MY POINT.
SO I'M GONNA END THIS RANT NOW,
AND GO AND RELAX WITH A JOINT.

BUT BEFORE I DO THAT, THOUGH,
JUST LET ME QUICKLY ADD THIS.
STOP USING BIG WORDS, AUTHORS,
BECAUSE YOU'RE TAKING THE BLOODY PISS!

CYSTS

I'D LIKE TO TALK ABOUT CYSTS NOW,
WHICH I'VE HAD ALL MY LIFE.
AND THEY'VE CAUSED ME ALL SORTS OF PROBLEMS,
AND NO SMALL AMOUNT OF STRIFE.

YOU SEE, THEY'RE GROWING ALL OVER MY BODY,
AND SEEM TO BE RUNNING RIFE.
AND THEY'VE EVEN FORCED ME ON SEVERAL OCCASIONS
TO GO UNDER THE KNIFE.

SO THE FIRST CYST I EVER NOTICED,
WAS BACK WHEN I WAS VERY YOUNG.
AND MY DOCTOR FROZE IT AND CUT IT OUT,
AND IT SURPRISINGLY BARELY STUNG.

AND THE CYST WAS IN MY RIGHT CHEEK,
AN INCH UNDER MY EYE.
AND I'VE STILL GOT THE SMALL SCAR
TO REMEMBER IT BY.

SO I'VE ALSO GOT ONE FLOATING IN MY JAW,
AND ONE ON MY RIGHT KNEE.
BUT THEY'RE NOT CAUSING ME ANY PROBLEMS,
AT LEAST NONE THAT I CAN SEE.

BUT THE ONES IN MY EARLOBES, THOUGH,
HAVE GIVEN ME ALL SORTS OF GRIEF.
WHICH IS WHY I WAS TWICE FORCED
TO SEEK SOME SURGICAL RELIEF.

YOU SEE, THEY FILL UP WITH INFECTED BLOOD,
AND THEN SUDDENLY EXPLODE.
MAKING A TERRIBLE MESS OF THE CEILING AND WALLS
IN MY HUMBLE ABODE.

AND I'M NOT JOKING ABOUT THE MESS,
AS MY CYSTS ERUPT WITH SUCH FORCE.
THAT THE ROOM MORE RESEMBLES AN ABATTOIR
WHERE THEY'VE JUST SLAUGHTERED A HORSE!

BEDWETTING

I DON'T DO THIS NOW. *HONEST!*
BUT I USED TO AS A KID.
AND THERE WAS NO RHYME OR REASON
FOR WETTING THE BED LIKE I DID.

AND I DIDN'T DO IT EVERY SINGLE NIGHT,
BUT IT WAS DEFINITELY MORE HIT THAN MISS.
WHICH IS WHY I BECAME USED TO SLEEPING
IN A PUDDLE OF MY OWN PISS.

SO MAYBE I WAS A SLOW LEARNER,
OR JUST EXERCISED POOR BLADDER CONTROL.
WHICH WAS WHY I NOCTURNALLY LEAKED URINE
FROM MY TINY MEAT POLE.

AND PERHAPS HAVING A MICROPENIS
WAS THE REAL ROOT OF MY TROUBLE.
AS I MAY'VE HAD A MATCHING TINY BLADDER,
THAT SUDDENLY BURST LIKE A BUBBLE.

BUT I GUESS THE REASON DOESN'T MATTER NOW,
AS THAT PROBLEM'S LONG GONE.
ALTHOUGH, IT COULD RETURN IN MY LATER YEARS,
AS I DECLINE INTO MY SWAN SONG.

AND I TRY NOT TO THINK ABOUT MY ENDING,
AS IT OBVIOUSLY MAKES ME UNHAPPY.
BUT I'D DEFINITELY HATE TO SPEND MY LAST FEW YEARS
WEARING AN INCONTINENCE NAPPY!

Lads' Holiday:

Darren went on his first lads' holiday to the Med
and spent day one getting pissed out of his head.
    All his mates got severely drunk too,
    but managed to make it to the loo,
whereas, Dazza just shat in his bed.

PHOBIAS

I'M AFRAID OF BEING STUNG,
LIKE I WAS AS A LITTLE KID.
WHEN MY HAND SWELLED UP LIKE A BALLOON,
AND I'M NOT LYING, IT REALLY DID.

AND THE BEE STING HURT LIKE HELL,
BUT THEN, I WAS ONLY ABOUT FIVE.
WHICH EXPLAINS WHY WHENEVER I HEAR BUZZING,
I NOW QUICKLY DUCK AND DIVE.

AND I'M ALSO AFRAID OF SPIDERS,
ALTHOUGH, THAT'S DEPENDANT ON THEIR SIZE.
BUT THEN, ANYTHING WITH MORE THAN FOUR LEGS
I'M QUITE HAPPY TO DESPISE.

AND THEN THERE'RE THE THINGS THAT HAVE NO LEGS,
LIKE SNAKES IN THE GRASS.
BUT THEN, ANY INSECT OR CREEPY-CRAWLY
I'M QUITE HAPPY TO BYPASS.

AND IT'S NOT JUST THE MULTITUDE OF LIVING THINGS,
WHICH CAN GIVE ME A FRIGHT.
AS THERE ARE A WHOLE BUNCH OF EXPERIENCES,
WHICH CAN MAKE ME TURN WHITE.

AND I REALLY HATE HEIGHTS, FOR EXAMPLE,
AND WALKING OVER BRIDGES.
AS WELL AS BEING COOPED UP IN TIGHT SPACES,
LIKE WARDROBES, LIFTS OR FRIDGES.

I ALSO DISLIKE WATCHING HORROR MOVIES,
BECAUSE I'M AFRAID OF THE DARK.
AND I EVEN GET A LITTLE ANXIOUS,
WHEN I HEAR A DOG BARK.

BUT IT ISN'T THE DOG I'M AFRAID OF
IT'S THE THOUGHT OF BEING BITTEN.
WHICH IS WHY I'VE NEVER OWNED A PUPPY,
OR EVEN A KITTEN.

NOW, I COULD KEEP ON GOING WITH THIS,
BUT WE'D BE HERE FOR QUITE A WHILE.
SO I'LL WRAP THINGS UP QUICKLY,
WHILE YOU'RE STILL WILLING TO SMILE.

AND I'M REALLY TERRIFIED OF GUNS,
WHICH IS WHY I'VE NEVER SHOT ONE AT GROUSE.
AND THEN THERE'S MY GROWING AGORAPHOBIA,
THAT'LL SOON STOP ME LEAVING THE HOUSE!

3 MISS RULE

THE THREE MISS RULE WAS ADDED TO SNOOKER,
IN ORDER TO SPEED UP PLAY.
WHICH, SEEMED LIKE A VERY SENSIBLE IDEA
AT THE END OF THE DAY.

BUT I'VE THOUGHT OF A PROBLEM, HOWEVER,
WHICH COULD LEAVE A PLAYER FEELING QUITE SICK.
BECAUSE, WHEN THEY'RE PLAYING THE THIRD SHOT,
WHAT HAPPENS IF THEY GET A NASTY, FATAL KICK?

SO NOW THE PLAYER'S LOST THE FRAME,
AND THROUGH NO REAL FAULT OF THEIR OWN.
WHICH SEEMS KINDA BLOODY HARSH TO ME,
AND RATHER DIFFICULT TO CONDONE.

AND THAT'S NOT ALL, MIND YOU,
AS THERE'S AN EVEN BIGGER CATCH.
BECAUSE, IF IT'S ALSO THE FINAL FRAME,
THEN THEY'LL LOSE THE FUCKING MATCH.

SO I'VE HAD A MUCH BETTER IDEA,
WHICH WILL REALLY SPEED UP PLAY.
GET RID OF THE MISS RULES ALTOGETHER,
WHICH IS AN EASY THING TO SAY.

BUT IT WOULD MAKE SNOOKER MORE FUN,
AND THE OVERALL GAME FAR MORE ATTACKING.
AND I'M SURE THAT MESSRS TRUMP AND O'SULLIVAN
WOULD GLADLY GIVE IT THEIR BACKING!

Snooker Player:

There's a Bristolian snooker player called *Judd Trump*
who likes to give the balls a good thump.
   He's had a great deal of general success,
   but in the *World Championship* far less,
and it's starting to give all his loyal fans the hump.

KARAOKE

KARAOKE WAS ORIGINALLY INVENTED
WAY BACK IN 1971.
BY SOME RANDOM GUY IN JAPAN
WHO THOUGHT IT'D BE FUN.

BUT WHAT'S FUN ABOUT LISTENING TO PEOPLE
WHO CAN'T SING A FUCKING NOTE.
AND IF THERE WAS A PETITION TO BAN KARAOKE,
IT WOULD GET MY BLOODY VOTE.

AND I'M FAR FROM THE ONLY PERSON
WHO THINKS THAT KARAOKE IS SHIT.
AS IT WAS RECENTLY VOTED THE UNITED KINGDOM'S
MOST HATED GADGET.

AND IT MAY BE FUN FOR THE SINGER
WHO'S HAD MORE THAN A FEW BEERS.
BUT IT'S NOT FUN FOR THE POOR AUDIENCE
WHO'RE ALL COVERING THEIR EARS.

AND THE SAME SONGS ARE BEING BUTCHERED
NO MATTER WHERE YOU GO.
IT'S LIKE OUR ANTISOCIAL BEHAVIOUR
HAS FINALLY HIT AN ALL-TIME LOW.

AND THERE'S "SWEET CAROLINE" AND "VALERIE",
AND THE INEVITABLE "DANCING QUEEN".
AND THEN SOME TOSSER WILL MANGLE "MY WAY",
JUST TO COMPLETE THE WAILING SCENE.

AND THESE PEOPLE WILL OFTEN SOUND
LIKE THEY'RE STRANGLING A CAT.
AND I JUST DON'T SEE WHERE THE FUN IS
IN HAVING TO LISTEN TO THAT.

AND I CAN'T EVEN VISIT MY LOCAL ANYMORE
FOR A QUIET PINT AND SOME GRUB.
WITHOUT SOME SHIT VERSION OF THE X FACTOR
TAKING OVER THE FUCKING PUB!

STICKY LABELS

I DON'T HATE ALL STICKY LABELS,
SO MOST FORMS OF THEM ARE ANGER EXEMPT.
BUT THERE IS A CERTAIN TYPE, THOUGH,
FOR WHICH I HAVE NOTHING BUT CONTEMPT.

AND THOSE ARE THE PRICE REDUCTION LABELS,
WHICH ARE USED TO GRAB OUR ATTENTION.
AND I WISH WITH ALL MY HEART
THAT THEY'D COME UP WITH A LESS STICKY INVENTION.

SO THE SHOPS PUT THEM ON EVERYTHING,
TO ENSURE THEY GARNER MANY LOOKS.
BUT WHAT PISSES ME OFF THE MOST,
IS WHEN THEY STICK THEM ON BOOKS.

AND THAT'S WHY BUYING A PRICE-REDUCED BOOK
ALWAYS FILLS ME WITH FEAR.
AS I KNOW THAT REMOVING THE STICKY LABEL
COULD EASILY CAUSE IT TO SMEAR.

AND THEN THE BOOK'S COVER WILL BE RUINED
WITH SOME DISCOLOURATION OR GLUE.
LEAVING ME BOTH IRATELY RED-FACED,
AND FEELING TERRIBLY BLUE.

BUT THE REAL PROBLEM, OF COURSE,
IS THAT I BITE MY FUCKING NAILS.
WHICH IS WHY REMOVING THOSE STICKY LABELS
ALWAYS EPICALLY FAILS!

Good Samaritan:

Gladys was a good Samaritan from Leeds
who was well-known for her kind-hearted deeds.
    She regularly helped to feed the poor
    and volunteered at a charity store
where she stole books that were considered good reads.

BEING STARTLED

NOW, WHEN IT COMES TO MY NERVES,
I'M A JITTERY FUCKER.
WHICH IS WHY BEING STARTLED
CAUSES MY ARSEHOLE TO PUCKER.

AND I'LL LITERALLY TWITCH OR JUMP
AT ANY UNEXPECTED NOISE.
WHICH IS A CONSTANT SOURCE OF AMUSEMENT
TO MY NEIGHBOUR'S TWO BOYS.

SO THEY'RE A PAIR OF VERY NAUGHTY RASCALS
WHO REALLY LOVE PLAYING TRICKS.
WHICH IS WHY MY SHREDDED NERVOUS SYSTEM
HAS TAKEN SOME SERIOUS LICKS.

AND I REALLY DETEST BEING STARTLED, OF COURSE,
BUT THAT DOESN'T STOP THE LITTLE TYKES.
WHICH IS WHY I RECENTLY GOT MY OWN BACK
BY REVERSING OVER THEIR NEW CHRISTMAS BIKES!

YOUTUBE ADVERTS

THERE'S NOTHING WORSE THAN CLICKING ON A VIDEO,
AND GETTING A FUCKING ADVERT, INSTEAD.
AND I NEVER KNOW WHEN IT'LL HAPPEN, OF COURSE,
UNTIL I'M ACTUALLY SEEING RED.

AND THEN I JUST SIT THERE FUMING,
WAITING FOR THE *SKIP* LINK TO APPEAR.
SO IT'S A BLOODY GOOD JOB, THEN,
THAT THERE AREN'T ANY SHARP OBJECTS NEAR.

AND I KNOW THAT FIVE MEASLY SECONDS
DOESN'T SEEM LIKE A GOOD REASON TO FLIP.
BUT IT'S STILL TIME I'VE FUCKING WASTED
WHEN I COULD HAVE BEEN WATCHING MY CLIP.

AND IT MAY NOT BE FIVE SECONDS, OF COURSE,
AS IT COULD BE THIRTY SECONDS OR MORE.
WHICH IS WHEN I GO SEARCHING FOR ANOTHER VIDEO,
BECAUSE I EASILY BORE!

NICKNAMES

I ABSOLUTELY HATE BLOODY NICKNAMES,
WHICH SHOULD COME AS NO REAL SURPRISE.
AS EVERY TIME I'M REFERRED TO AS "DICK",
A TINY PIECE OF ME DIES.

AND I HOPED I'D BE CALLED "JET" AT SCHOOL,
AS MY INITIALS ARE J-E-T.
BUT THEY ALL SHORTENED MY NAME TO JON,
WHICH JUST BEGAN MY MISERY.

SO IT WASN'T LONG BEFORE THE OTHER KIDS LEARNED
THAT JON THOMAS WAS A SLANG TERM FOR DICK.
AND THEN THAT'S WHAT THEY ALWAYS CALLED ME,
WHEN THEY WEREN'T USING THE TERMS "PENIS" OR "PRICK".

BUT IT WASN'T JUST THE OTHER KIDS, THOUGH,
THAT I HAD TO PUT UP WITH AT SCHOOL.
AS ALL THE SNIGGERING TEACHERS DURING ROLLCALL
WERE JUST AS DAMN CRUEL.

AND I BLAME MY PARENTS, OF COURSE,
I MEAN, WHAT THE HELL WERE THEY THINKING?
BUT MAYBE THEY THOUGHT IT'D BE FUNNY,
OR PERHAPS THEY'D BEEN DRINKING.

AND I SUPPOSE THERE'S A SLIGHT CHANCE, OF COURSE,
THAT THEY DIDN'T KNOW WHAT THEY WERE DOING.
BUT THEIR TERRIBLE CHOICE STILL PISSES ME OFF,
AND MAKES ME FEEL LIKE FUCKING SUING!

Maths Teacher:

Bethany was a stout maths teacher with bad breath
whose every utterance smelled just like death.
    She also had sweaty pits,
      which got on her students' tits,
so they nicknamed the tubby bitch "Stinky Beth".

JUGGLING

NOW, I DON'T WANT TO BRAG,
OR SOUND LIKE A COMPLETE DICK.
BUT I'M REALLY GOOD AT JUGGLING,
AND I MEAN SERIOUSLY SLICK.

AND I CAN JUGGLE ANY THREE OBJECTS,
WHICH I CAN HOLD WITH MY HANDS.
AND I'VE MET MOST OF MY SELF-IMPOSED CHALLENGES,
AND OTHER PEOPLES' DEMANDS.

I'VE ALSO LEARNT TO DO A NUMBER OF TRICKS, TOO,
NOT THAT I CAN REMEMBER THEIR NAMES.
BUT I ALMOST PRACTISE THEM AS MUCH
AS PLAYING MY VIDEO GAMES.

AND I CAN EVEN THROW A BALL OVER MY SHOULDER,
AND CATCH IT UNSEEN BEHIND MY BACK.
WHICH SHOULD CERTAINLY HELP TO CONVINCE YOU
THAT I'M NOT SOME SORT OF A HACK.

AND IF THAT HASN'T MADE YOU A BELIEVER,
THEN LET ME FURTHER MAKE MY POINT.
AS I WAS ONCE DARED TO JUGGLE THREE WHITE MICE,
WHILE WE WERE PASSING ROUND A JOINT.

SO I QUICKLY JUMPED UP TO MY FEET,
TOOK THE CHALLENGE, AND DIDN'T LINGER.
AND EVERYTHING WENT QUITE SMOOTHLY
UNTIL ONE OF THE LITTLE BUGGERS BIT MY FINGER.

AND I KNOW WHAT YOU'RE THINKING NOW,
BUT WHAT HAPPENED TO THE POOR MICE?
BUT I WAS SAFELY JUGGLING THEM OVER A BED,
SO THEIR LANDING WAS CUSHIONED AND NICE!

Children's Clown:

Mr. Chuckles was a cheery children's clown from Yuma
who slowly lost his great sense of humour.

He gradually grew sicker,

feared it was his ticker,

but tests showed it was an inoperable tumour.

SLEEPWALKING

I ONCE LIVED WITH A GUY THAT SLEEPWALKED,
AND OUR RELATIONSHIP WAS PLATONIC NOT RUDE.
BUT UNFORTUNATELY FOR ME, THOUGH,
HE LIKED TO SLEEP IN THE NUDE.

AND THAT LED TO SOME SLEEPWALKING MOMENTS,
WHICH WERE SERIOUSLY DISTRESSING.
AS SEEING ANOTHER GUY'S SHRIVELLED JUNK
IS ALWAYS A SIGHT THAT'S AWKWARD AND DEPRESSING.

BUT HE HAD A SMALL DICK, HOWEVER,
AND HIS PUBES WERE QUITE BUSHY AND BIG.
SO IT WAS MORE LIKE LOOKING
AT AN EXTREMELY BAD WIG.

AND HE DIDN'T KNOW HE WAS DOING IT, OF COURSE,
SO I COULDN'T GET TOO MAD.
UNTIL I POLITELY ASKED HIM TO SLEEP IN HIS BOXERS,
AND HE TOLD ME, *"TOO BAD!"*

AND THAT REALLY UPSET ME, OF COURSE,
HIS JUST DISMISSIVELY SAYING NO.
WHICH IS WHY I PROMPTLY DECIDED
TO PUT AN END TO THE PEEP SHOW.

SO I QUICKLY FOUND ANOTHER PLACE TO LIVE,
AND WITH A YOUNG WOMAN THIS TIME.
AS I FIGURED THAT WATCHING HER NUDE SLEEPWALKING
WOULD FEEL LIKE LESS OF A CRIME!

Sleepwalker:

There once was a frequent sleepwalker called Jude
who wandered all around his hometown of Bude.
  But the poor guy didn't know,
  'til he stubbed his toe,
and woke up outside in the nude.

ULCER

THEY SAY THAT STRESS IS A SILENT KILLER,
BUT IT HASN'T DONE ME IN YET.
THOUGH, IT HAS GIVEN ME AN ULCER,
WHICH HAS INCREASED HOW MUCH I FRET.

AND MY DOCTOR SAID IT ISN'T BLEEDING,
EVEN THOUGH IT HURTS LIKE BLOODY HELL.
THEN HE PRESCRIBED ME SOME GASTRO CAPSULES,
WHICH SHOULD SOON MAKE ME FEEL WELL.

NOW, I DON'T USUALLY TRUST MY DOCTOR,
AS HE'S BEEN KNOWN TO BE WRONG.
BUT I'M NOT SHITTING BLOOD YET,
DESPITE THE GOD-AWFUL PONG.

SO MAYBE HE'S GOT THIS ONE RIGHT FOR A CHANGE,
AND I TRULY HOPE THAT HE HAS.
BECAUSE MY STOMACH PAIN IS CHRONIC,
THOUGH, NOT AS UNCOMFORTABLE AS JAZZ.

AND THE DOC PROMISED THAT AFTER TAKING THE MEDICATION,
I'D BE AS FIT AS A HORSE.
BUT I CAN ONLY TAKE ONE PILL A DAY, THOUGH,
SO IT'LL TAKE NEARLY A MONTH TO FINISH THE COURSE.

AND FOUR WEEKS IS AN AWFULLY LONG TIME
FOR ME TO BE IN CONSTANT GASTRIC PAIN.
SO I HOPE THE PILLS DO THE TRICK,
AND THAT ALL THIS EXTRA STRESS HASN'T BEEN IN VAIN!

Henpecked Husband:

There was a henpecked husband from Wyoming called Brett
whose growing ulcer was making him upset.
　So he killed his bitching wife with a shovel,
　buried her in Lovell,
and got himself a far more affectionate pet.

INSOMNIA

IT'S ANOTHER NIGHT OF TOSSING AND TURNING,
AND BEING UNABLE TO SLEEP.
AS MY INSOMNIA'S DRIVING ME CRAZY,
AND MAKING ME WEEP.

AND IT'S BEEN THREE WEEKS SINCE I LAST SLEPT,
WHICH IS TWENTY-ONE NIGHTS IN A ROW.
AND I SIMPLY CAN'T TAKE IT ANYMORE,
SO TO MY DOCTOR I GO.

SO I TELL THE DOC ABOUT MY ROOT-CANAL INFECTION,
WHICH GOT MY RESTLESSNESS STARTED.
AND HE PRESCRIBES A SHORT COURSE OF SLEEPING PILLS,
AND THEN I QUICKLY DEPARTED.

SO THE PILLS THANKFULLY DID THE TRICK,
AND I FINALLY GOT SOME MUCH-NEEDED REST.
BUT MY INSOMNIA SOON REARED ITS UGLY HEAD AGAIN,
LIKE AN UNWANTED PEST.

YOU SEE, SLEEPING PILLS ARE VERY ADDICTIVE,
AND THUS CAN'T BE TAKEN FOR VERY LONG.
WHICH MEANT I NEEDED A MORE PERMANENT SOLUTION,
BEFORE THINGS BEGAN GOING WRONG.

SO MY DOCTOR STUDIED MY NOTES AGAIN,
AND THEN HE HAD AN IDEA THAT WAS BRIGHT.
AND HE PRESCRIBED ME A STRONG ANTIDEPRESSANT,
WHICH WOULD HAVE ME OUT LIKE A LIGHT.

NOW, I KNOW THIS IDEA SEEMS CRAZY,
BUT IT'S NOT AS MAD AS YOU MIGHT THINK.
AS I WAS ALREADY SUFFERING FROM DEPRESSION,
AS WELL AS NOT SLEEPING A WINK.

SO THE ANTIDEPRESSANTS WORK REALLY WELL,
AND NOW I HAPPILY SLEEP LIKE A LOG.
BUT I'M STILL ABLE TO WAKE DURING THE NIGHT
IN CASE I NEED TO NIP TO THE BOG!

FAKE TAN

I DON'T GET PEOPLE WHO USE FAKE TAN,
BECAUSE IT NEVER LOOKS RIGHT.
IT LOOKS LIKE THEY'VE BEEN SPRAYED ORANGE
IN THE MIDDLE OF THE NIGHT.

AND WHAT'S WRONG WITH BEING PASTY,
AND VERY PALE AND WHITE?
AND LOOKING LIKE SOMEONE WHO'S JUST SUFFERED
A TERRIBLE FRIGHT?

AND FAKE TAN IS SOLD IN MANY FORMS,
AND EVEN COMES WITH AN APPLICATION MITT.
BUT REGARDLESS OF THE PRODUCT USED,
IT STILL LOOKS LIKE COMPLETE SHIT.

AND I KNOW THAT SUNBEDS ARE DANGEROUS,
BUT SO'S RUBBING TOXIC CHEMICALS INTO THE SKIN.
SO WHEN IT COMES TO LOOKING BRONZED ALL YEAR ROUND,
YOU JUST CAN'T FUCKING WIN.

AND I GET THAT PEOPLE WANT TO LOOK GOOD,
AND THAT THEY WANT TO BE SEEN.
BUT, SURELY, NOT AT THE COST
OF LOOKING LIKE A BAKED BEAN!

TAXIDERMY

THIS IS YET ANOTHER STRANGE PRACTICE
THAT I'VE NEVER REALLY UNDERSTOOD.
EVEN WHEN IT'S DONE BY A TRUE ARTIST,
AND TURNS OUT REALLY GOOD.

AND I GET KEEPING STUFFED ANIMALS IN MUSEUMS,
IN ORDER TO PRESERVE HISTORY.
BUT WHY PEOPLE WOULD WANT THEM IN THEIR HOMES
IS A TOTAL FUCKING MYSTERY.

AND I DON'T SEE THE POINT OF KEEPING A PET
LONG AFTER IT'S DIED.
BY GUTTING IT AND CLEANING IT,
AND THEN STUFFING ITS HIDE.

AND THERE'S JUST SOMETHING ABOUT THE EYES,
WHICH MAKES THE POOR ANIMAL POUT.
PLUS, THEY'RE BEADY AND KIND OF WEIRD,
AND THEY REALLY CREEP ME OUT!

HOOVERING

I'VE GOT A CUTE *"HENRY"* HOOVER,
WHICH IS COLOURED BRIGHT RED.
BUT I'M STILL CONSIDERING SWAPPING HIM
FOR A NEW *DYSON*, INSTEAD.

YOU SEE, HE'S VERY CUMBERSOME TO USE,
AND ATTACHED TO A RESTRICTIVE CORD.
AND HE ALSO BUMPS INTO THINGS,
WHICH IS WHY I'M GROWING SO BORED.

AND I KNOW HE'S A MEMBER OF THE FAMILY,
AND THAT HE HAS A SWEET FACE.
BUT HE'S REALLY SHOWING HIS AGE NOW,
AND FALTERING IN THE HOOVERING RACE.

AND HE'S NOT THAT AGILE ANYMORE, EITHER,
AND BLOWS A LOT OF DUSTY, HOT AIR.
WHICH UPSETS MY NUMEROUS ALLERGIES,
AND INCREASES MY REASONS NOT TO CARE.

BUT IT'S HIS SERIOUS LACK OF SUCTION,
WHICH IS WHY I THINK THAT *HE SUCKS*.
AND THE MAIN REASON WHY I'M CONTEMPLATING
SHELLING OUT THE BIG BUCKS.

AND I COULD BUY SOMETHING LIGHT AND CORDLESS,
WHICH'LL HELP WITH THE MANOEUVRING.
BUT I SERIOUSLY DOUBT IT'LL CHANGE THE FACT,
THAT I REALLY HATE FUCKING HOOVERING!

Modern Dancer:

Mallory was a modern dancer based in Vancouver
who was a beautiful, rhythmical mover.
    She was light on her feet,
    could dance to any beat,
and always practised her cha-cha with the hoover.

203

RUNNING COMMENTARY

I HATE PEOPLE WHO PROVIDE A RUNNING COMMENTARY
ON EVERYTHING THEY DO.
AND EVEN IF THEY'RE NOT AWARE OF IT,
IT'S STILL FUCKING DIFFICULT TO CHEW.

AND ALTHOUGH I SAID CHEW,
I REALLY WANTED TO SAY SWALLOW.
BUT THAT WOULDN'T HAVE RHYMED, OF COURSE,
WHICH IS WHY I LEFT IT TO FOLLOW.

ANYWAY, LET'S GET BACK TO THE CONSTANT TALKERS,
AND THEIR VERBAL DIARRHOEA.
WHICH I DETEST WITH MY WHOLE BEING,
AND OBVIOUSLY DON'T WANT TO HEAR.

AND THEY'RE CONSTANTLY STATING THE FUCKING OBVIOUS,
LIKE IT'S RAINING OR IT'S COLD.
AND I ALWAYS KNOW WHAT THE BLOODY WEATHER'S DOING
WITHOUT BEING SODDING TOLD.

SO THEIR POINTLESS, BANAL WITTERING
SOON DRIVES ME TO DISTRACTION.
AND I HAVE TO WORK HARD NOT TO STRANGLE THEM,
OR SHOW ANY SORT OF REACTION.

BUT THEY'RE TOO BUSY TO SEE MY FRUSTRATION, THOUGH,
BY BEING A CONSTANT SPEAKING CLOCK.
SO ALL I CAN DO IS QUIETLY FANTASISE
ABOUT GAGGING THEM WITH A SOCK.

NOW, I COULD MOAN ABOUT THIS FOR AGES,
BUT THAT WOULDN'T BE FAIR TO YOU.
SO I'M GOING TO START TO WRAP THINGS UP
BY NAMING MY WORST TWO.

AND I KNOW WHEN SOMEONE GRABS THEIR MUG
THAT THEY'RE GOING TO MAKE A BREW.
SO I DON'T NEED TO BE FUCKING TOLD THIS,
NOR WHEN THEY'RE JUST POPPING TO THE LOO.

AND NOW FOR THE FINAL TWO VERSES,
WHICH MAY POSSIBLY OFFEND.
THOUGH, I GUESS ON YOUR SENSE OF HUMOUR
THAT'LL ACTUALLY DEPEND.

AND MY MOTHER'S ONE OF THESE PEOPLE,
WHICH OBVIOUSLY MAKES HER DIFFICULT TO AVOID.
AND GUARANTEES HER NUMEROUS VISITS TO MY HOME
ARE MORE ANNOYING THAN A HAEMORRHOID!

KARMA

DO YOU BELIEVE IN THE EXISTENCE OF KARMA,
AND ITS ASSOCIATED SCALE?
WELL I CERTAINLY DO,
HENCE WHY I'M PENNING THIS SHORT TALE.

BUT I DON'T BELIEVE THE SCALE'S BALANCED, THOUGH,
BECAUSE THAT SIMPLY ISN'T THE CASE.
AS THERE ARE THE FEW WHO HAVE EVERYTHING,
AND THEN THERE'S THE REST OF THE HUMAN RACE.

AND I HAVE TO BELIEVE SOMEONE'S GETTING THE GOOD STUFF,
BECAUSE I'M CERTAINLY NOT.
WHICH IS THE ONLY THING THAT'S STOPPING ME
FROM COMPLETELY LOSING THE PLOT.

AND I'M SURE YOU'VE HEARD OF THE SAYING,
"GETTING THE SHIT END OF THE STICK".
WHICH BASICALLY SUMS UP MY WHOLE LIFE,
AND I'M NOT DELIBERATELY LAYING IT ON THICK.

AND IT HASN'T BEEN ALL SHIT, OF COURSE,
BUT THERE'S DEFINITELY BEEN MORE BAD THAN GOOD.
WHICH, GIVEN MY TIMID NATURE,
I'VE NEVER REALLY UNDERSTOOD.

AND I'VE ALWAYS TRIED TO DO THE RIGHT THING,
AND NOT FUCK ANYONE IN THE ASS.
AND THE RESULT OF ALL THAT EFFORT
IS A LIFE THAT'S BARELY BEEN THIRD CLASS.

AND AREN'T THE MEEK SUPPOSED TO INHERIT THE EARTH,
WHICH IS WHAT I'VE ALWAYS HEARD?
BUT THE ONLY THING I'VE SEEMINGLY INHERITED
IS THE ABILITY TO RHYME ANY WORD.

AND PERHAPS THAT'S BEEN THE PROBLEM
THAT I WASN'T DOING SOMETHING I TRULY LOVE.
SO NOW THAT I'M WRITING AMUSING RHYMES,
MAYBE MY KARMA WILL GET A POSITIVE SHOVE!

DETENTION

IT'S VERY LATE ON A SATURDAY NIGHT,
AND I FIND MYSELF THINKING ABOUT DETENTION.
AND WHETHER I CAN SQUEEZE A FUN RHYME OUT OF IT,
OR IF I SHOULD EVEN GIVE IT A MENTION.

AND I NEVER UNDERSTOOD BEING KEPT BACK AFTER SCHOOL,
IN ORDER TO PAY MY DUE.
AS IT ALWAYS SEEMED LIKE THE SUPERVISING TEACHER
WAS BEING PUNISHED, TOO.

AND THE TEACHER WATCHING OVER ME
WAS NEVER THE ONE THAT I OFFENDED.
WHICH IS SOMETHING ELSE I NEVER UNDERSTOOD,
THOUGH, MAYBE THAT WAS INTENDED.

AND THEN THERE WAS WRITING SODDING LINES,
WHICH I HAD TO DO OVER AND OVER.
WHICH SEEMED LIKE SUCH A POINTLESS TASK,
AND A POOR PROBLEM SOLVER.

AND HOW THE BLOODY HELL WAS WRITING
"I MUST NOT SWEAR AT MY TEACHER" A THOUSAND TIMES.
SUPPOSED TO BE A SENSIBLE AND BEFITTING PUNISHMENT
IN RELATION TO MY COMMITTED CRIMES.

AND I ALSO WASN'T ALLOWED TO SPEAK,
AND HAD TO SPEND THE WHOLE DETENTION IN SILENCE.
WHICH WAS SUCH A MINOR THING TO SUFFER,
AFTER COMMITTING AN ACT OF MILD VIOLENCE.

SO, NOW IT'S THE EARLY HOURS OF SUNDAY MORNING,
AND I STILL HAVEN'T WRITTEN ANYTHING FUNNY.
WHICH MEANS THIS'LL BE YET ANOTHER SILLY RHYME,
THAT DOESN'T MAKE ME ANY MONEY.

AND PERHAPS MY TIME WOULD HAVE BEEN BETTER SPENT,
ATTENDING THE LOCK-IN AT THE LOCAL PUB.
OR MAYBE I SHOULD'VE RHYMED ABOUT THAT FILM INSTEAD
YOU KNOW, THE ONE ENTITLED *"THE BREAKFAST CLUB"!*

COLD

MY COLD STARTS WITH A SLIGHT COUGH,
AND A BIT OF A SCRATCHY THROAT.
BUT THERE'S FAR WORSE TO COME,
AS THAT'S NOT ALL SHE WROTE.

AND AS MY THROAT GROWS SORER,
IT'S JOINED BY A BUNGED UP NOSE.
WHICH MAKES ME SOUND COMPLETELY RIDICULOUS
AS IT GARBLES MY PROSE.

AND I'M NOT LOOKING FORWARD TO WORK,
AS I KNOW I'LL BE ASKED TO SPEAK.
AND THE MEETING WILL BE A DISASTER,
THANKS TO MY VERY CONGESTED BEAK.

NOW, THERE'S NO CURE FOR THE COMMON COLD,
BUT THAT DOESN'T STOP ME FROM TRYING.
AS I'D PREFER TO QUICKLY FEEL BETTER,
AND NOT LIKE I'M DYING.

SO I PICK UP SOME COLD TREATMENTS AND MEDICINES
ON MY WAY TO WORK.
BUT AS SOON AS MY COLLEAGUES SEE ME TAKING THEM
THEY ALL GO BERSERK.

AND THEY SUDDENLY TREAT ME LIKE I'M A LEPER,
LIKE I'VE GOT THE BLACK PLAGUE.
AND ALL MY REASSURANCES OTHERWISE
COME OUT MUFFLED AND VAGUE.

AND THEY KNOW I'VE GOT THE LURGY,
IT'S AS PLAIN AS THE RUNNY NOSE ON MY FACE.
WHICH IS WHY THEY'RE ALL FLEEING FROM ME,
LIKE I'VE JUST FALLEN FROM SPACE.

AND THEY OBVIOUSLY DON'T WANT TO BE AROUND ME,
AND CAN'T WAIT TO GET AWAY.
AS THEY'RE DESPERATE NOT TO CATCH
WHATEVER'S CAUSING MY FACIAL DECAY.

SO MY HEAD IS SOON FILLED WITH COTTON WOOL,
AND I'M STARTING TO SWEAT.
AND I'VE GOT NO IDEA HOW MUCH WORSE
MY SYMPTOMS WILL ACTUALLY GET.

SO I DRINK ANOTHER HOT *LEMSIP*,
AND SWALLOW SOME MORE PILLS.
AND THEN I SIT STEWING IN MY CHAIR
WHILE I GO GREEN AT THE GILLS!

211

HEADACHE

IT BARELY EVEN REGISTERS
WHEN I CRAWL OUT OF BED.
JUST THE MEREST HINT OF AN ACHE
IN THE BACK OF MY HEAD.

SO I TRY TO PUSH IT FROM MY MIND,
AND GET ON WITH MY DAY.
BUT I INSTINCTIVELY KNOW THAT MY HEADACHE
ISN'T GOING AWAY.

SO BY THE TIME I GET TO WORK,
MY HEAD IS BEGINNING TO THROB.
BUT I JUST MAKE MYSELF A COFFEE,
AND GET ON WITH MY JOB.

AND ALTHOUGH THE NEXT FEW HOURS PASS QUICKLY,
THE PAIN SLOWLY GETS WORSE.
SO I RUMMAGE THROUGH MY DESK,
AND THEN LET OUT A CURSE.

NOW, I THOUGHT I HAD SOME PARACETAMOL,
BUT MUST HAVE GIVEN THEM AWAY.
WHICH CAUSES THE THROBBING TO BECOME LOUDER,
MUCH TO MY DISMAY.

SO I ASK AROUND THE OFFICE,
BUT ONLY COME UP WITH SOME ASPIRIN.
WHICH WILL DO LESS THAN SOD ALL
TO ALLEVIATE THE PULSATING DIN.

SO NOW I HAVE TO SUFFER UNTIL LUNCHTIME,
AND THEN I RUSH OUT TO *BOOTS*.
WHERE I BUY SOME PARACETAMOL AND CODEINE
TO ATTACK THE PROBLEM AT ITS ROOTS.

AND THE CODEINE BLOCKS PAIN RECEPTORS,
AND SHOULD GET TO WORK IN A FEW HOURS.
AND THEN I'LL BE BACK TO FEELING NORMAL,
AND AT THE HEIGHT OF MY POWERS.

BUT MY LUCK ISN'T IN, THOUGH,
AND THE BLOODY PILLS DON'T DO THE TRICK.
AND THE PAIN JUST KEEPS ON ACHING,
AND GETTING RIGHT ON MY WICK.

SO I SLOG MY WAY BACK HOME AFTER WORK,
AND WATCH TV WHILE GETTING MYSELF FED.
WHERE MY HEADACHE EVENTUALLY SUBSIDES
JUST IN TIME FOR FUCKING BED!

HYPOCHONDRIA

THE FACT THAT I SUFFER FROM HYPOCHONDRIA
SHOULD REALLY COME AS NO SURPRISE.
AS I'VE BEEN SICK FOR MOST OF MY LIFE,
AND IT'S SWIFTLY HASTENING MY DEMISE.

AND MY DOCTOR SAYS THAT I'M IMAGINING IT,
AND THAT IT'S ALL IN MY HEAD.
BUT I WONDER IF HE'LL CHANGE HIS TUNE
ONCE I'M UNABLE TO GET OUT OF BED.

SO I THINK I'M ILL WHEN I'M NOT,
AND APPARENTLY IT'S ALL IN MY MIND,
AND IT'S NOT LIKE I'M STUPID,
OR BEING DELIBERATELY BLIND.

BECAUSE I KNOW WHAT I'M FEELING,
AND IT SEEMS VERY REAL.
BUT IF I CAN'T TELL THE BLOODY DIFFERENCE,
THEN HOW AM I SUPPOSED TO HEAL.

NOW, PERSONALLY, I THINK IT'S AN ANXIETY DISORDER,
AS I'M ANXIOUS ALL THE TIME.
AND I'M EVEN WORRYING RIGHT NOW,
WHILE I COMPOSE THIS LITTLE RHYME.

YOU SEE, THIS RHYME'S SUPPOSED TO BE AMUSING,
BUT IT'S NOT EVEN CLOSE.
AND HOW AM I SUPPOSED TO CHEER YOU UP,
WHEN I FEELING SO MOROSE.

AND THEN THERE'S MY EMOTIONAL ROLLERCOASTER,
WHICH MAKES VERY LITTLE SENSE.
AS I RANDOMLY SWITCH FROM BEING HAPPY TO SAD,
TO FEELING INCREDIBLY TENSE.

AND AS WELL AS MY CRAZY MOOD SWINGS,
I GET THIS FEELING OF BEING TRAPPED.
BUT THEN, PERHAPS IT TRULY IS ALL IN MY HEAD,
AND I'M JUST TOO TIGHTLY WRAPPED!

CALM DOWN!

I REALLY HATE BEING TOLD TO CALM DOWN
WHEN I'M GENUINELY UPSET.
SO I'LL HAPPILY TELL THAT PERSON TO FUCK OFF
WITHOUT ANY REGRET.

AND I'M AGITATED FOR A VALID REASON,
AND DON'T WANT IT TO BE DOWNPLAYED.
AS IT FURTHER AGGRAVATES MY NERVES,
WHICH ARE ALREADY FRAYED.

AND THEN THERE'S THE FACT THAT IT'S CONDESCENDING,
AS WELL AS CLICHÉD AND LAZY.
NOT TO MENTION THAT IT INSINUATES,
THAT I MIGHT JUST BE CRAZY.

AND THEN THERE'S ALSO THE PROBLEM,
THAT I DON'T LIKE BEING TOLD WHAT TO DO.
AND I'M SURE YOU CAN UNDERSTAND THAT,
AND HAVE PROBABLY BEEN THERE, TOO.

SO I'LL DO THE EXACT OPPOSITE, OF COURSE,
AND BECOME EVEN MORE STRESSED.
AND THEN I'LL FEEL LIKE I'M BEING JUDGED,
AND GROW A LITTLE DEPRESSED.

AND IF THINGS KEEP GETTING WORSE,
THEN I'LL NEED A RELEASE.
BUT EVEN VENTING MY BOILING ANGER
WON'T BRING ME MUCH PEACE.

SO THE NEXT TIME YOUR PARTNER'S UPSET,
HERE'S A USEFUL LITTLE TIP.
THAT'LL HELP TO EASE THE SITUATION,
AND ALLOW THEM TO GET A GRIP.

AND YOU NEED TO BE CARING AND SYMPATHETIC,
AND ASK THEM WHAT'S WRONG.
WHICH'LL STOP THEM FROM GOING CRAZY
AND TURNING INTO KING KONG!

CHIN UP!

I HATE BEING TOLD TO KEEP MY CHIN UP
BY SOME INSENSITIVE BOOR.
WHICH IS WHY HEARING SAID WORDS
ALWAYS SPARKS A VERBAL WAR.

AND I'M DEALING WITH SOME SERIOUS HEALTH ISSUES,
AND HAVE A RIGHT TO OCCASIONALLY FEEL DOWN.
WHICH IS WHY I SHOULDN'T HAVE MY SAD FEELINGS NEGATED
BY SOME POSITIVE ARSECLOWN.

AND I'M NOT LOOKING FOR ANY SYMPATHY,
OR FOR PEOPLE TO ENQUIRE WHY I'M SAD.
I JUST WANT TO BE LEFT ALONE NOW AND THEN,
SO I CAN WALLOW AND FEEL BAD.

AND I KNOW IT'S NOT FUN FOR THE PEOPLE AROUND ME,
WHEN I SIT AROUND AND BROOD.
BUT I'M SUFFERING EVERY DAY,
AND HAVE EARNED THE RIGHT TO BE IN A FOUL MOOD!

SHITTY SHOE

IT OBVIOUSLY GOES WITHOUT SAYING
THAT THIS IS AN UNPLEASANT EVENT.
AND ONE I'M SURE WE ALL TAKE STEPS
TO HOPEFULLY PREVENT.

BUT IN SPITE OF OUR BEST EFFORTS, THOUGH,
WE STILL OCCASIONALLY RUN AFOUL.
AND THERE'S NOTHING LIKE GETTING A SHITTY SHOE
TO GENERATE A VERY LIVID SCOWL.

AND THIS HAPPENS TO ME MORE OFTEN
THAN I'D ACTUALLY LIKE TO ADMIT.
AS THE CANAL BANK I WALK ALONG
IS PRACTICALLY COVERED IN DOGSHIT.

AND THE STUFF EVEN HIDES UNDER LEAVES,
LIKE IT'S WEARING A DISGUISE.
JUST WAITING FOR ME TO STEP IN IT,
AND GET THAT FUCKING SHITTY SURPRISE!

THE LAST WORD

PEOPLE WHO MUST HAVE THE LAST WORD
FILL ME WITH IRRATIONAL HATRED AND RAGE.
AND IF YOU'RE ONE OF THESE PEOPLE,
THEN I SUGGEST YOU TURN THE FUCKING PAGE.

BECAUSE THIS RHYME ISN'T GOING TO BE COMPLIMENTARY,
AND YOU CAN FUCKING BANK ON THAT.
SO EITHER MOVE ALONG RIGHT NOW,
OR STRAP ON YOUR HARD HAT.

AND THESE ARSEHOLES JUST ARGUE AND ARGUE,
UNTIL THEY EVENTUALLY WIN.
AND I GET SO SICK OF LISTENING TO THEM,
THAT I JUST PREFER TO GIVE IN.

AND THEY ALSO TALK FASTER AND LOUDER
TO GET THEIR POINT ACROSS.
WHICH IS WHY I LOSE THE WILL TO LIVE,
AND DON'T GIVE A FLYING TOSS.

AND THEY THINK THEY KNOW EVERYTHING,
AND THEY THINK THEY'RE ALWAYS RIGHT.
AND I JUST HAVE TO LEAVE THE ROOM,
SO I DON'T SET THEM ALIGHT.

NOW, I WOULD NEVER DO THAT, OF COURSE,
AS I'VE GOT WAY TOO MUCH CLASS.
BUT THAT DOESN'T STOP ME FROM CONSIDERING IT
WHILE THEY'RE TALKING OUT THEIR ASS.

AND I'VE GOT ONE FINAL THING TO SAY
TO ALL THOSE MUPPETS WHO MUST HAVE THE LAST WORD.
TAKE A FUCKING CHILL-PILL FOR CHRIST'S SAKE,
AND STOP BEING SO ANNOYING AND ABSURD!

SECURITY LIGHTS

NOW, I KNOW THEY SERVE AN IMPORTANT PURPOSE,
AND I DON'T WANT TO SOUND LIKE A PUTZ.
BUT WHEN IT COMES TO EXTERNAL SECURITY LIGHTS,
THEY JUST DRIVE ME FUCKING NUTS.

AND BEFORE YOU THINK THAT I'M CRAZY,
AND JUST QUIETLY SCOFF.
I'M TALKING ABOUT THE MOTION-ACTIVATED ONES,
WHICH NEVER SEEM TO TURN OFF.

AND MY NEIGHBOUR'S GOT ONE OF THESE, OF COURSE,
AND IT BURNS VERY BRIGHT.
AND THAT'S THROUGH MOST OF THE DAY,
AND THEN THE BLOODY NIGHT.

AND IT'S LIKE HAVING A SODDING LIGHTHOUSE
STUCK RIGHT OUTSIDE MY FUCKING ROOM.
AND EVEN A SET OF VERY HEAVY CURTAINS
DON'T GUARANTEE ME SOME GLOOM.

AND THINGS HAVE GOTTEN SO BAD LATELY,
THAT I'M CONSIDERING TAKING SOME ACTION.
THOUGH, YOU'LL PROBABLY THINK THAT MY PLAN
IS A BIT OF AN OVERREACTION.

SO I'M CONSIDERING SHOOTING IT WITH MY AIR RIFLE,
AS IT NEVER SEEMS TO FAIL.
BUT THEN, KNOWING MY TERRIBLE LUCK
I'D END UP IN FUCKING JAIL!

Night Light:

Toby had trouble getting to sleep every night
due to a lamppost that burned very bright.
    He complained to the council quite often,
    but the bulb's glow they wouldn't soften,
so he got an air rifle and shot out the light.

REALITY TV

I'D LIKE TO WRITE SOMETHING REALLY SCATHING
ABOUT REALITY TV.
ESPECIALLY ALL THE TEDIOUS DRIVEL
SUCH AS, *MADE IN CHELSEA*.

AND I'D ALSO LIKE TO EXPLAIN,
HOW IT FILLS ME WITH INEXPLICABLE RAGE.
AS WELL AS WHY THE PEOPLE CREATING IT
SHOULD BE LOCKED IN A CAGE.

AND WHILE I GENUINELY DO BELIEVE,
THAT MOST OF THE REALITY SHOWS ARE SHIT.
TO ACTUALLY NAME ANY MORE NAMES
WOULD MAKE ME A HYPOCRITE.

AND THE REASON FOR THAT, OF COURSE,
IS BECAUSE I WATCH SOME OF THE SHOWS.
THOUGH, I DOUBT THEY'RE ONES YOU'VE HEARD OF,
BUT WE'LL SEE HOW IT GOES.

SO THEY'RE SHOWN ON THE *DISCOVERY* AND *HISTORY*
CHANNELS,
STRAIGHT FROM THE USA.
BUT THEY'RE STARTING TO APPEAR ON THE MAINSTREAM
CHANNELS, TOO,
THAT WE WATCH EVERY DAY.

AND THE SHOWS ARE MOSTLY ABOUT FINDING THINGS,
OR CREATING CUSTOM CARS.
SO STUFF LIKE, *AUCTION HUNTERS*, *FAST 'N' LOUD*,
AND THE AMUSING VEGAS *PAWN STARS*.

AND YOU'VE ALSO GOT *STORAGE WARS*, *BITCHIN' RIDES*,
AND THOSE *AMERICAN PICKERS*.
AND THEN THERE'S THE HILARIOUS *DUCK DYNASTY*,
WHICH CAN CREATE WET KNICKERS.

THERE'S ALSO *COUNTING CARS* AS WELL,
WHICH IS ANOTHER ENTERTAINING FIND.
AND THERE ARE PROBABLY ONE OR TWO OTHERS,
WHICH HAVE CURRENTLY SLIPPED MY MIND.

NOW, I DON'T KNOW HOW MY SHOWS STACK UP
AGAINST ALL THE OTHER REALITY FARE.
BUT THEN, GIVEN I DON'T WATCH ANY OF THAT STUFF
I DON'T ACTUALLY CARE.

AND I CAN'T SEE THE POINT OF WATCHING THE *KARDASHIANS*,
OR ANY OF THOSE *REAL HOUSEWIVES*.
WHO JUST KEEP WASTING OUR PRECIOUS TIME
BY FILMING THEIR SUPERFICIAL LIVES!

TOOTHACHE

I HATE GOING TO THE DENTIST, OF COURSE,
BUT I HATE DENTAL PAIN MORE.
WHICH, AT ITS MOST EXTREME,
CAN HAVE ME WRITHING ON THE FLOOR.

AND IT ALWAYS STARTS AT THE WORST POSSIBLE TIME,
LIKE LATE ON A FRIDAY NIGHT.
SO I HAVE TO SUFFER THROUGH THE WEEKEND
BEFORE I CAN SEEK SOME RESPITE.

AND IT USUALLY BEGINS WITH A TWINGE,
WHEN I DRINK SOMETHING HOT.
BUT I KNOW THAT'S JUST THE BEGINNING,
AND IT'S GOING TO HURT QUITE A LOT.

SO THE TWINGE RAPIDLY BECOMES AN ACHE,
WHICH THEN TURNS INTO A SOLID THROB.
AND PRETTY SOON ALL I CAN THINK ABOUT
IS THE PULSATING AGONY IN MY GOB.

SO I SWALLOW SOME PAIN PILLS,
BUT THEY DON'T MAKE A DENT.
WHICH LEAVES ME PULLING OUT MY HAIR,
AND NEEDING TO VENT.

THEN SOMEONE SUGGESTS HAVING A DRINK,
SO I BREAK OUT THE BOOZE.
AND I KNOW I SHOULDN'T MIX THE TWO,
BUT I'VE GOT NOTHING TO LOSE.

SO I SWIFTLY THROW BACK SOME DRINKS,
AND THEN I'M SOON DRUNK *AND* IN PAIN.
AND THEN I DECIDE TO KEEP GOING,
SO ALL MY EFFORTS WON'T BE IN VAIN.

AND IT ISN'T LONG BEFORE I PASS OUT,
AND THEN DRIFT OFF TO SLEEP.
AND I'D BEST MAKE THE MOST OF IT
BEFORE THE PAIN RUNS TOO DEEP.

SO I SLOG MY WAY THROUGH THE WEEKEND,
WHICH IS TWO DAYS OF TORTUROUS HELL.
AND THEN I CALL THE DENTAL SURGERY ON MONDAY MORNING,
WITH MY PAINFUL TALE TO TELL.

SO I BEG THEM FOR AN EMERGENCY APPOINTMENT,
AS I CAN'T STAND THE PAIN ANYMORE.
AND THEN THEY CALMLY EXPLAIN THEY'RE FULLY BOOKED
UNTIL NEXT BLOODY FRIDAY AT FOUR!

227

DENTISTS

I'VE ALREADY COVERED THE SUBJECT OF "TOOTHACHE"
IN MY PREVIOUS KINDLE BOOK CALLED: *SICK*.
BUT THAT STILL LEAVES ME WITH ANOTHER BONE
THAT I ACTUALLY NEED TO PICK.

AND THIS MAY NOT RING ANY BELLS WITH YOU,
BUT IT'S CERTAINLY ANNOYING ME.
SO I HOPE YOU'LL KEEP ON READING
TO FIND OUT WHAT THAT ISSUE MIGHT BE.

AND THAT BONE HAS TO DO WITH MONEY,
WHICH SEEMS SUCH AN OBVIOUS THING TO SAY.
BUT BEFORE MY DENTIST WILL ACTUALLY TREAT ME,
HE REQUIRES ME TO BLOODY PAY.

SO ARE YOU AWARE OF THIS NEW POLICY, THEN,
AND DOES IT HAPPEN TO YOU?
AND DOES IT ALSO LEAVE YOU SCRATCHING YOUR HEAD,
AND FEELING PISSED OFF, TOO?

AND I REALLY DON'T UNDERSTAND PRE-PAYING
BEFORE MY DENTIST WILL COME OUT AND PLAY.
UNLESS HE'S WORRIED THAT AFTER HIS POOR TREATMENT
I'LL FUCK HIM OVER AND RUN AWAY!

WRONG LIGHTBULBS

PURCHASING THE WRONG TYPE OF LIGHTBULB
IS GUARANTEED TO RUIN MY FUCKING DAY.
BUT I NEVER NOTICE MY MISTAKE, THOUGH,
UNTIL I TRY AND PUT THE BASTARD INTO PLAY.

AND THEN I'M LEFT STANDING IN THE DARK,
AND SCREAMING A BLOODY RACKET.
BUT IT'S MY OWN FUCKING FAULT, OF COURSE,
FOR NOT DOUBLE-CHECKING THE PACKET.

AND WHY CREATE TWO DIFFERENT FITMENTS
IN THE SODDING FIRST PLACE?
AND WHICHEVER BASTARD CREATED THE SECOND ONE
SHOULD BE SHOT IN THE FACE.

AND I KNOW THAT BLOODY BAYONET BULBS
CAN OFTEN BE QUITE FIDDLY TO FIT.
BUT CREATING THE SECOND SCREW-IN TYPE
REALLY WAS JUST POINTLESS AND SHIT!

FLU

MY FLU STARTS JUST LIKE A COLD,
BUT THEN SWIFTLY GETS MUCH WORSE.
AND IT SOON HAS ME LAID UP IN BED,
AND PUTS ALL MY PLANS IN REVERSE.

AND IT ALSO COMES WITH A HACKING, WET COUGH,
AND A PHLEGMY, CONGESTED CHEST.
WHICH MAKES IT VERY HARD TO BREATHE,
AND ROBS ME OF REST.

SO MY ILLNESS QUICKLY BUILDS TO A LEVEL,
WHICH IS MORE THAN I CAN BEAR.
AND NOT ONLY DOES MY WHOLE BODY ACHE,
BUT I'VE ALSO GOT PAINFUL HAIR.

AND I KNOW THAT SOUNDS CRAZY,
BUT MY HAIR'S PAINFUL TO TOUCH.
SO I QUICKLY PRAY FOR SLEEP,
AS IT'S ALL BECOME JUST TOO MUCH.

SAID SLEEP NEVER ARRIVES, THOUGH,
BUT I DO GET THE HOT AND COLD SHIVERS.
AND WHEN I'M NOT FREEZING MY TITS OFF,
I'M SWEATING FUCKING RIVERS.

SO I THINK ABOUT CALLING THE DOCTOR,
BUT I'M NOT A BIG BELIEVER.
AND THEN I TRY TO REMEMBER THAT RHYME
ABOUT FEEDING A COLD AND STARVING A FEVER.

SO THE TERRIBLE FATIGUE SETS IN NEXT,
AND SOON MY TEMPERATURE IS SOARING.
AND I'D GIVE ANYTHING RIGHT NOW
TO BE FAST ASLEEP AND SNORING.

BUT I'VE ALSO GOT A BAD HEADACHE,
AND A NASTY, SORE THROAT.
AND THEN THERE'S THE FOUL TASTE IN MY MOUTH,
LIKE I'VE JUST SUCKED OFF A GOAT.

SO THERE'S NOTHING LEFT TO DO NOW
BUT HOPE THAT MY FLU BURNS ITSELF OUT.
THOUGH, IT DOESN'T SEEM THAT LIKELY,
AND GIVES ME MUCH CAUSE FOR SELF-DOUBT.

SO I SWALLOW SOME MORE PARACETAMOL,
AND GULP DOWN SOME MORE WATER.
AND THEN I WAIT FOR THE FLU TO RAVAGE MY ACHING BODY,
LIKE A LAMB TO THE SLAUGHTER!

SPOTS

I GO TO BED BLEMISH FREE,
BUT I WAKE UP WITH A SPOT.
AND I KNOW THE LITTLE SUCKER'S THERE
BEFORE I'VE EVEN ROLLED OUT OF MY COT.

AS I CAN FEEL ITS TERRIBLE, UNWANTED PRESENCE,
HERALDED BY THAT UNMISTAKABLE SLIGHT PAIN.
SO I DASH TO THE NEAREST MIRROR
TO CHECK OUT THE EXTENT OF THE STAIN.

AND I CAN SEE THE LITTLE DEVIL QUITE CLEARLY,
RIGHT BETWEEN MY WEAK CHIN AND LOWER LIP.
WHICH IS THE PERFECT CENTRALISED LOCATION
TO ENSURE EVERYONE NOTICES MY GREASY BLIP.

BUT IT'S THANKFULLY QUITE SMALL.
ALTHOUGH, IT'S STILL VERY VISIBLY RED.
AND GROWING RIGHT AT ITS CENTRE
IS THE BEGINNING OF A TINY YELLOW HEAD.

NOW, MY FIRST INSTINCT IS TO SQUEEZE IT,
BUT I DON'T WANT THE INFECTION TO SPREAD.
SO I QUASH MY POPPING DESIRE,
AND REACH FOR MY TUBE OF *FREEDERM* INSTEAD.

AND I KNOW THE GEL WON'T STOP IT FROM GROWING,
BUT IT MIGHT REDUCE THE REDNESS A BIT.
AND I'D SETTLE FOR ANYTHING RIGHT NOW
TO DISGUISE THE EXISTENCE OF MY ZIT!

New Pimple:

Annabelle woke up to find she had a new pimple
and knew squeezing it wouldn't be simple.
It was at the bottom of her face,
stuck in a really weird place,
slap-bang in the middle of a dimple.

HAY FEVER

SUMMER IS COMING,
NOT THAT I ACTUALLY CARE.
AS IT'LL TRIGGER MY HAY FEVER,
AND CAUSE IT TO FLARE.

AND I'LL SOON HAVE ITCHY EYES,
AND A RED STREAMING NOSE.
WHICH'LL DEPRESS ME TO THE CORE,
AND AFFECT MY ABILITY TO DOZE.

AND I'M ALREADY TAKING MY PILLS,
BUT THEY'RE NEVER A HUNDRED PER CENT.
AND ON THE REALLY BAD POLLEN DAYS,
THEY HARDLY MAKE A DENT.

SO I HOPE THE SUMMER WILL BE OVER QUICKLY,
OR AT LEAST VERY MILD.
AS I'M SICK OF DEALING WITH MY HAY FEVER,
WHICH I'VE HAD SINCE A CHILD.

YOU SEE, IT'S LIKE HAVING A COLD FOR SEVEN MONTHS,
AND NOT AT ALL A FUN RACE.
AS I'LL BE SPENDING A GREAT DEAL OF THAT TIME
WITH A TISSUE STUCK TO MY FACE.

AND AS FOR THE SLEEPLESS NIGHTS,
THERE ARE JUST WAY TOO MANY TO COUNT.
AND THEN THERE'S MY DISAPPROVING GIRLFRIEND,
WHOM I'M NOT ALLOWED TO MOUNT.

AND I EVENTUALLY GET SO FED UP,
THAT I BEG MY DOC FOR SOMETHING MUCH STRONGER.
BUT HE JUST SHAKES HIS HEAD, THOUGH,
AND SAYS THE REALLY GOOD STUFF ISN'T MADE ANY LONGER.

AND HE EXPLAINS THAT THE BEST STUFF WAS FATAL,
AND LINKED TO CAUSING HEART ATTACKS.
SO I'M STUCK WITH THE CRAP PILLS I'VE ALREADY GOT
IN THEIR FIDDLY BLISTER PACKS!

PARKING SPACES

I COULD COMPLAIN ABOUT THE COST OF USING CAR PARKS,
BUT THIS ISN'T THE TIME OR THE PLACE.
AND BESIDES, I'D MUCH RATHER BITCH ABOUT
NOT BEING ABLE TO FIND A FUCKING SPACE.

AND I END UP DRIVING AROUND IN BLOODY CIRCLES
AT A MORE AND MORE FURIOUS PACE.
PRAYING I'LL BE THE ONE TO FIND AN EMPTY SPOT
IN AN EVER DIMINISHING RACE.

AND WHY DOES EVERYONE RUSH INTO TOWN
AT THE SAME FUCKING TIME AS ME?
COULDN'T THEY JUST WAIT AN EXTRA HOUR
BEFORE STARTING THEIR SHOPPING SPREE?

AND I JUST WANT TO GET MY HAIR CUT,
AND MAYBE POP INTO THE BANK.
AND I HARDLY EVER USE THE WHOLE HOUR, EITHER,
WHICH IS ANOTHER THING THAT'S WANK.

SO WHY CAN'T THEY CREATE A FAIRER SYSTEM,
WHERE WE ONLY PAY FOR THE TIME WE ACTUALLY USE.
AS PEOPLE WOULD RELINQUISH THEIR SPACES MUCH SOONER,
ONCE THEY'D FINISHED SHOPPING FOR SHOES.

236

BUT THEY WANT TO GET VALUE FOR MONEY THOUGH,
SO THEY USE THE WHOLE SODDING HOUR.
WHICH IS WHY I CAN NEVER FIND A FREE SPACE,
AND THE PARKING EXPERIENCE MAKE'S ME SO BLOODY SOUR!

WAITING FOR DELIVERIES

I CAN'T STAND WAITING FOR DELIVERIES
WHERE THEY ONLY SPECIFY MORNING OR AFTERNOON.
AS I KNOW THEY'LL ALWAYS SHOW UP MUCH LATER
RATHER THAN HELPFULLY SOON.

AND THEN I JUST HAVE TO MOOCH AROUND THE HOUSE,
GETTING MORE AND MORE BORED.
AND EVEN WHEN I FINALLY GET THE DELIVERY,
IT DOESN'T FEEL LIKE MUCH OF A REWARD.

SO I CAN'T REALLY RELAX OR FULLY SETTLE,
UNTIL THE DOORBELL ACTUALLY RINGS.
AND I CAN SEE THAT IT'S THE DELIVERY GUYS,
BRINGING ME MY ORDERED THINGS.

BUT UNTIL THAT HAPPENS, OF COURSE,
I HAVE TO TRY AND NOT LOSE MY MIND.
WHILE I JUST SIT STARING AT THE CLOCK,
AND WATCH TIME SLOWLY GRIND.

BUT IT ISN'T REALLY THE WAITING THAT PISSES ME OFF
IT'S ACTUALLY ALL THE TIME I HAVE TO WASTE.
BECAUSE I'M DEALING WITH SLOW PEOPLE
WHO DON'T UNDERSTAND THE CONCEPT OF HASTE.

AND I HAVE TO TAKE TIME OFF FROM WORK, TOO,
WHICH ONLY MAKES MATTERS WORSE.
AS THAT'S A PRECIOUS AMOUNT OF MY HOLIDAY,
THAT NO ONE WILL EVER REIMBURSE!

Delivery Guy:

There once was a delivery guy called Stan
who died after a crash in his van.
    But the poor bloke wasn't driving;
    he was actually muff-diving
in the back with a woman named Fran.

CELEBRATIONS

THINK MINIATURE CHOCOLATES, NOT PARTIES,
AND YOU'LL GET WHERE I'M COMING FROM.
AND I HONESTLY BELIEVE THAT *CELEBRATIONS*
ARE THE CHOCCY PINNACLE OF YUM.

AND YOU GET EIGHT FAMOUS BRANDS,
ALL INDIVIDUALLY WRAPPED TO STAY FRESH.
WHICH I'M HAPPY TO KEEP GOBBLING,
WITH SCANT REGARD FOR MY FLESH.

SO LET'S GO THROUGH THEM IN ORDER, THEN,
AND WE'LL START WITH THE DELICIOUS *TWIX*.
WHICH IS THE FIRST ONE I ALWAYS REACH FOR,
WHEN I NEED A CONFECTIONARY FIX.

BUT YOU DON'T GET MANY IN A CARTON, THOUGH,
WHICH ALWAYS LEAVES ME FEELING BLUE.
AND EVEN THE BIGGER CHRISTMAS TUBS,
ONLY HAVE A MEAGRE FEW.

SO NEXT IS THE MINI *MARS BAR*,
WHICH IS A SMALL PIECE OF SILKY HEAVEN.
AND YOU GET CONSIDERABLY MORE OF THESE,
SOMETIMES AS MANY AS SEVEN.

AND THEN THERE'S THE *MILKY WAY*,
WHICH YOU MAY THINK IS A SIMILAR PLAYER.
BUT THE WHIPPED CENTRES ARE VERY DIFFERENT,
AND THERE'S NO CARAMEL LAYER.

SO THE MINIATURE *SNICKERS* COMES NEXT,
COMPLETE WITH ITS TINY CHOPPED NUTS.
AND IT ONLY TAKES A MERE SAVOURY SECOND
FOR IT TO SLIP DOWN INTO MY GUTS.

THEN THERE'S THE ODD SHAPED *MALTESER*
WITH ITS YUMMY BISCUIT BITS.
BUT IT WAS THE RECENT SIZE REDUCTION OF THE CARTONS
WHICH HAD ME IN FITS.

AND THERE'S ALSO THE *BOUNTY* TO CONSIDER,
WHICH GETS STUCK BETWEEN MY TEETH.
A SMOOTH MILK CHOCOLATE COVER
WITH MOIST COCONUT BENEATH.

AND FINALLY, THERE'S THE *GALAXY* AND *CARAMEL*
WHICH ARE MY LEAST FAVOURITE TWO.
THOUGH, I SOON FORGET THAT LITTLE FACT
WHEN I'M HUNTING FOR SOME SCRUMMY CHOCOLATE TO
CHEW!

ADDICTION

I'VE DEVELOPED A VERY SERIOUS ADDICTION,
BUT IT'S NOT WHAT YOU'RE THINKING.
AS IT'S GOT NOTHING TO DO WITH TAKING DRUGS,
OR SMOKING, OR DRINKING.

AND DESPITE MY LOVE OF TELEVISION,
IT'S NOT EVEN WATCHING TV.
AS I'M ADDICTED TO COLLECTING FILMS
THAT'VE BEEN RELEASED ON DVD.

AND WHEN I SAY DVD,
I OF COURSE MEAN BLU-RAY AS WELL.
AND I'M JUST UNABLE TO HELP MYSELF,
IT'S LIKE I'M UNDER A SPELL.

AND I REALLY LOVE WATCHING FILMS,
AND COULD EASILY WATCH THEM ALL DAY.
AS THEY ALLOW ME TO ESCAPE FROM REALITY,
AND JUST GET AWAY.

SO IF YOU'VE READ THE RHYME I WROTE CALLED: *FILMS*,
IN MY FIRST KINDLE BOOK OF RHYMES CALLED: *LIFE*.
THEN YOU'LL KNOW I'VE GOT NEARLY A THOUSAND FILMS NOW,
WHICH IS MUCH CHEAPER THAN A WIFE.

AND I'VE ONLY BEEN BUYING THEM FOR SIXTEEN YEARS,
SO I'LL LET YOU DO THE MATH.
AND THE ONLY TIME I'M NOT WATCHING THEM
IS WHEN I'M SLEEPING OR TAKING A BATH!

Film Industry:

The film industry has hit an all-time low
by releasing an emoji movie, don't you know?
    And I honestly consider this
    to be taking the piss,
not that that'll stop people wanting to go.

ALLERGIES

NOW, I KNOW I'VE ALREADY COVERED HAY FEVER,
BUT THERE ARE MILLIONS OF ALLERGIES.
AND SOME OF THEM CAN EVEN KILL YOU,
LIKE EATING NUTS OR STINGING BEES.

BUT MOST ARE FAIRLY MILD, THOUGH,
NOT THAT THAT MAKES THEM DESIRED.
AND I ONCE KNEW A GUY WITH A WORK ALLERGY,
WHICH SOON GOT THE POOR BUGGER FIRED.

BUT SERIOUSLY, SOME ALLERGIES CAN MAKE YOU SICK,
WHILE OTHERS CAN GIVE YOU SPOTS.
AND SOME CAN SCREW WITH YOUR INTESTINES,
AND GIVE YOU THE TROTS.

AND SOME CAN ALSO CAUSE REACTIONS,
LIKE RASHES AND HIVES ON YOUR SKIN.
WHICH ARE SO FRIGGING ITCHY,
YOU DON'T KNOW WHERE THE SCRATCHING SHOULD BEGIN.

AND MY PARENTS ACTUALLY MADE ME GET TESTED
WAY BACK WHEN I WAS A KID.
AND THE MILLIONS OF POSITIVE RESULTS
CAUSED ME TO COMPLETELY BLOW MY LID.

SO THE LENGTHY LIST STARTED WITH MILK,
AND THEN SOMETHING CALLED AZO DYES.
BUT IT WAS REALISING I COULDN'T HAVE CHOCOLATE,
THAT BROUGHT THE TEARS TO MY EYES.

AND THE LIST WAS SO RIDICULOUSLY LONG,
THAT IT WENT FROM THE CEILING TO THE FLOOR.
SO I JUST STORMED OUT OF THE ROOM,
AS I COULDN'T BEAR TO HEAR ANY MORE.

AND I DECIDED IT WAS BEST NOT TO KNOW,
AND JUST TREAT THE WHOLE THING AS MENTAL.
AS THERE WERE BOUND TO BE THINGS I'D NEVER EAT,
LIKE THE POOR, HUMBLE LENTIL.

I'M NOT SURE THAT WAS A SMART MOVE, THOUGH,
AS I'VE BEEN ILL FOR MOST OF MY LIFE.
BUT KEEPING MILLIONS OF ALLERGIES STRAIGHT,
JUST SEEMED LIKE WAY TOO MUCH STRIFE.

THOUGH, I DO TRY TO AVOID THE BAD ONES,
THE WORST OF WHICH IS MILK.
BUT I'LL BE DAMNED IF I'M GIVING UP CHOCOLATE,
WHICH IS THE SWEETIE EQUIVALENT OF SILK!

MIGRAINE

MY MIGRAINE BEGINS LIKE A HEADACHE,
AND THEN IT CRIPPLES MY BRAIN.
AND I'M UNABLE TO THINK CLEARLY,
BECAUSE OF THE INTENSE BURST OF PAIN.

SO I QUICKLY SWALLOW TWO CODEINE PILLS,
BUT THEY DON'T DO THE TRICK.
AND THE PAIN KEEPS GETTING WORSE,
AND MAKES ME MENTALLY SICK.

AND IT FEELS LIKE SOMEONE'S DRILLING A HOLE,
THROUGH THE TOP OF MY SKULL.
AND I'D GIVE ANYTHING FOR SOME RELIEF,
OR EVEN A MOMENTARY LULL.

BUT THE PRESSURE KEEPS ON BUILDING,
AND I KNOW IT'S NOT GOING TO DROP.
SO I'LL HAVE TO DO SOMETHING DRASTIC,
IF I WANT THE PAIN TO SUDDENLY STOP.

SO I TAKE FOUR MORE CODEINE PILLS,
WHICH TAKES MY CURRENT TOTAL TO SIX.
AND I DON'T CARE ABOUT THE SIDE EFFECTS,
AS I'M DESPERATE FOR A FIX.

YOU SEE, I JUST WANT THE INCESSANT PAIN TO STOP,
BEFORE IT MAKES MY HEAD IMPLODE.
AND I'M NOT THINKING ABOUT KIDNEY DAMAGE,
OR THE OTHER ORGANS THE DRUGS MIGHT ERODE.

SO AFTER THAT, I CRAWL INTO BED,
EVEN THOUGH IT'LL BE IMPOSSIBLE TO FIND SLEEP.
AS THE PAIN'S FAST REACHING A LEVEL,
THAT WILL CAUSE ME TO WEEP.

AND THEN I CONSIDER RENDERING MYSELF UNCONSCIOUS
MIGHT JUST BE THE WAY.
AS WAKING UP PAIN FREE
WOULD BE WORTH SACRIFICING A WHOLE DAY.

SO I SWALLOW SIX MORE CODEINE PILLS,
AND THEN WAIT FOR THAT COMATOSE BLISS.
AS I'M PERFECTLY HAPPY TO RISK WAKING UP
IN A PUDDLE OF MY OWN PISS!

ACNE

NOW, I KNOW I'VE ALREADY COVERED SPOTS,
BUT ACNE IS MUCH, MUCH WORSE.
AND I SPENT MOST OF MY TEENAGE YEARS
DEALING WITH THIS HARSH FACIAL CURSE.

AND I KNOW THIS IS A SERIOUS SUBJECT,
AND NOT ONE TO BE MADE AMUSING.
BUT I THINK I'VE EARNED THE RIGHT TO,
AS I'VE ALREADY SUFFERED THE ABUSING.

SO SCHOOL AND COLLEGE WEREN'T MUCH FUN FOR ME,
DUE TO THE AMOUNT I GOT TEASED.
AND THE NAME-CALLING WAS RELENTLESS,
UNTIL MY ACNE EVENTUALLY EASED.

SO I WAS CALLED SPOTTY AND CRATER-FACE,
TO NAME JUST A FEW.
AND THE OTHER KIDS NEVER GREW TIRED OF REMINDING ME,
THAT I WAS SPOILING THEIR VIEW.

AND IT'S NOT LIKE IT WAS MY FAULT, OF COURSE,
AS I WAS AT THE MERCY OF MY HORMONES.
WHICH WERE MORE INTENT ON GROWING RED BLOTCHES
THAN STRENGTHENING MY BONES.

AND THEN THERE WERE MY ALLERGIES,
WHICH PROBABLY DIDN'T HELP.
AND NOR DID ANY OF THE HERBAL REMEDIES I TRIED,
NOT EVEN THE KELP.

AND I REALLY THOUGHT MY PROBLEMS WOULD BE OVER,
ONCE MY ACNE HAD CLEARED.
BUT IT LEFT ME WITH POCKMARKS AND SCARS,
WHICH IS WHY I NOW HIDE BEHIND A BEARD!

Spotty Texan:

This is the bumpy tale of a spotty Texan called Doyle
who made an absolute fortune drilling for oil.
Now, you'd think he'd be happy
being such a rich chappy,
but all his zits were the size of a boil.

BEING UNPREPARED

I REALLY DESPISE PEOPLE WHO ARE UNPREPARED
FOR THE EVENTS THEY KNOW ARE DUE TO OCCUR.
AND IT'S JUST FURTHER PROOF IF PROOF'S NEEDED,
THAT PEOPLE ARE STEADILY GROWING DUMBER.

AND THE CLASSIC IS THE PERSON WITH THE MISLAID TICKET
WHO'S HOLDING UP THE ENTIRE FUCKING TRAIN.
AND WHEN THEY COME TO EXIT THE STATION LATER
YOU KNOW THEY'LL HAVE MISPLACED IT AGAIN.

AND THEN THERE'S THE PERSON IN THE CAR PARK
TRYING TO SCROUNGE UP THE CORRECT CHANGE.
AND IF THEY'RE STUPID ENOUGH TO ASK ME,
THEN I'LL GLADLY START A HEATED EXCHANGE.

SO I'LL ASK THEM WHY THEY'VE COME TO THE CAR PARK,
WITHOUT HAVING THE CORRECT MONEY.
AND IT WON'T TAKE THEM LONG TO REALISE,
THAT I'M NOT DELIBERATELY BEING FUNNY.

BUT IT DOESN'T JUST HAPPEN WITH CASH OR TICKETS,
AS THERE'RE ALSO PASSPORTS AND INVITATIONS.
AND THIS KIND OF UNPREPARED STUPIDITY
HAS BEEN GOING ON FOR GENERATIONS.

AND I CAN UNDERSTAND WOMEN LOSING STUFF
IN THEIR HUGE HANDBAGS FULL OF CRAP.
BUT IT'S THE GUYS LOSING ITEMS IN THEIR WALLETS,
WHICH CAUSES ME TO FUCKING SNAP!

UNRELIABLE PEOPLE

PEOPLE WHO NEVER DO WHAT THEY SAY THEY WILL,
REALLY GET ON MY TITS.
THEY DRIVE ME FUCKING CRAZY,
TO THE END OF MY WITS.

AND THEY ARRANGE TO MEET AT A SET TIME,
AND THEN SHOWUP NEARLY AN HOUR LATE.
AND THEY DON'T SEEM TO UNDERSTAND, EITHER,
WHY THIS MAKES ME SO BLOODY IRATE.

BUT IT'S WHEN THEY CANCEL PLANS AT THE LAST MINUTE
THAT I GO TOTALLY INSANE.
AND THEN THEY ACT ALL HURT AND INNOCENT
WHEN I FUCKING COMPLAIN.

AND THEY REALLY DON'T GET THE REASON
FOR MY SUDDEN OUTBURST OF EMOTION.
AS THEY JUST THINK I'M BEING CHILDISH,
AND CAUSING A POINTLESS COMMOTION.

BUT IT'S THE UNRELIABLE PEOPLE AT WORK
WHO FUCKING ANNOY ME THE MOST.
AND I WONDER HOW THEY GOT PAST THE INTERVIEW
WHEN THEY'RE SO SHIT AT THEIR POST.

AND THEY DO THE BARE MINIMUM EVERY DAY,
AND JUST GO THROUGH THE MOTION.
WHILE I'M SERIOUSLY BUSTING MY ARSE
TRYING TO EARN A VALUABLE PROMOTION!

Smart Skiver:

There once was a smart skiver named Kirk
who fancied another day off work.
    So he filled his bladder real quick
    to employ an old lying trick
and then he phoned in sick with a smirk.

FREERUNNING

THIS SPORT ISN'T FOR THE FAINTHEARTED,
OR FOR THOSE AFRAID OF HEIGHTS.
AS TACKLING ANY URBAN ASSAULT COURSE
COULD PRODUCE SOME VERY SCARY SIGHTS.

AND IT ACTUALLY ORIGINATED IN FRANCE,
WHERE THEY REFER TO IT AS PARKOUR.
BUT REGARDLESS OF HOW YOU PRONOUNCE IT,
IT'S STILL MIND-BLOWINGLY HARDCORE.

AND I LOVE WATCHING THE BEST ATHLETES
SHOW-OFF THEIR AMAZING SKILL.
AS WELL AS MARVELLING AT THEIR NERVES,
AND THEIR IRON SELF-WILL.

AND I WOULDN'T ATTEMPT FREERUNNING MYSELF,
AS I'M TOO BLOODY SCARED.
BUT I'M GLAD THAT THERE'RE OTHERS OUT THERE
WHO'VE ACTUALLY DARED.

AND I THINK ITS RECENT-ISH INVENTION
SAYS A LOT ABOUT THE HUMAN RACE.
THAT WE'RE STILL PUSHING THE ENVELOPE
AT SUCH AN INCREDIBLE PACE.

AND WE'RE ALWAYS LOOKING FOR NEW WAYS
TO SHOWCASE OUR ACROBATIC SKILLS.
REGARDLESS OF THE PERSONAL DANGER,
AND THE POTENTIAL FOR SPILLS.

AND YOU MAY THINK THIS SPORT IS POINTLESS,
AND WONDER WHY I'M MAKING SUCH A FUSS.
BUT A BIT OF FREERUNNING COULD PROVE VERY USEFUL
THE NEXT TIME YOU'RE LATE FOR THE BUS!

HIGH HEELS

NOW, I KNOW THAT BROACHING THIS SUBJECT
MAY NOT BE POLITICALLY CORRECT.
BUT I CAN ASSURE YOU THAT I'M DOING IT
WITH THE UTMOST RESPECT.

AND I JUST WANT TO ASK A QUICK QUESTION
THAT'LL ONLY TAKE TWO SECS.
WHICH IS, HOW DO WOMEN WALK IN HIGH HEELS
WITHOUT BREAKING THEIR NECKS?

AND I'M BEING DEADLY SERIOUS ABOUT THIS,
AND I'M NOT TAKING THE PISS.
AS I WOULD GENUINELY LIKE TO BE TOLD
THE ANSWER TO THIS.

AND THEY ALL WALK WITH SUCH EASE,
AND SEEM TO SHOW NO CONCERN.
SO IS THIS SKILL SOMETHING THEY'RE BORN WITH,
OR IS IT SOMETHING THEY LEARN?

AND I GUESS IT COULD BE GENETIC LIKE BREATHING,
OR LEARNT LIKE RIDING A BIKE.
AND THEN I WONDER IF WEARING HIGH HEELS
IS SOMETHING WOMEN EVEN LIKE.

BUT I'M SURE THEY DO, THOUGH,
AS THEY REALLY LOVE SHOPPING FOR SHOES.
WHICH IS WHY THEY ALWAYS HAVE MORE PAIRS
THAN THEY CAN EVER POSSIBLY USE!

Married Crossdresser:

Malcolm was a married crossdresser from Fife
who always borrowed clothes from his wife.
    He'd put on nice shoes and a tight dress,
    leave her underwear drawer in a mess,
and then go out and live his other life.

COUGH

I REALLY HATE GETTING A COUGH,
BECAUSE I ALWAYS DEVELOP A SORE THROAT.
AND REGARDLESS OF WHICH TYPE I GET,
I ALWAYS END UP IN THE SAME BOAT.

AND THE COUGH COULD BE TICKLY OR DRY,
OR CHESTY OR HACKING.
BUT I ALWAYS REACH FOR THE COUGH SYRUP
TO FINALLY SEND IT PACKING.

THE MEDICINE NEVER WORKS RIGHT AWAY, THOUGH,
SO I HAVE TO LIVE WITH MY COUGH.
AND I JUST KEEP ON COUGHING AND COUGHING,
UNTIL I PISS MYSELF OFF.

AND THEN THERE'S MY POOR THROAT,
WHICH STEADILY GROWS SORER.
BECAUSE MY ANNOYINGLY PERSISTENT COUGH
IS RUBBING IT RAWER.

SO I THINK THAT THE TICKLY OR DRY COUGHS
ARE ACTUALLY THE BEST ONES TO HAVE.
AS THEY USE THE LEAST AMOUNT OF TISSUES,
OR TOILET ROLL FROM THE LAV.

THEY'RE ALSO THE EASIEST ONES TO MANAGE
ON A DAY-BY-DAY BASIS.
AND THEREFORE PROVIDE THE LEAST DISRUPTION
TO MY HOMEOSTASIS.

BUT HAVING A CHESTY OR HACKING COUGH
IS LIKE CARRYING AROUND A PHLEGMY PEST.
AS THE INFECTION WORMS ITS WAY DEEPER,
AND GETS SERIOUSLY LODGED IN MY CHEST.

PLUS, THERE'S THE FACT THAT EVERY TIME I COUGH,
IT FEELS LIKE I'M TRYING TO BRING UP A LUNG.
AND THEY ALSO TAKE MORE TIME TO GO AWAY NOW,
BECAUSE I'M NO LONGER THAT YOUNG!

SHORT-SIGHTED

TO SAY THAT I'M SHORT-SIGHTED,
IS BEING SOMEWHAT OVERLY KIND.
AS WITHOUT MY CORRECTIVE GLASSES,
I'D BE CONSIDERED LEGALLY BLIND.

AND I'VE WORN SPECS SINCE I WAS SEVEN,
WHICH MY PARENTS USED TO GET FROM THE *NHS*.
AND THAT'S STILL VERY PAINFUL TO REMEMBER,
AND EVEN HARDER TO CONFESS.

SO THE LENSES WERE LIKE MILK BOTTLE BOTTOMS,
AND GAVE ME BIG EYES LIKE A FISH.
AND ADDING THE CHEAP PLASTIC FRAMES
MADE THEM THE SIZE OF A SATELLITE DISH.

AND THEN THERE WAS THE NAME-CALLING,
OF WHICH MY PARENTS NEVER KNEW.
STUFF LIKE, *SPECCY, FOUR-EYES, JOE-90,*
AND THE OBLIGATORY *MR. MAGOO.*

AND AS FOR SWITCHING TO CONTACT LENSES,
I DID GIVE THEM A DECENT TRY.
BUT I COULDN'T GET PAST THE CONSTANT DISCOMFORT
OF HAVING SOMETHING STUCK IN MY EYE.

AND LASER SURGERY WAS IN ITS INFANCY BACK THEN,
AND NOT MANY PEOPLE DARED.
AND I NEVER EVEN CONSIDERED IT,
AS I WAS TOO FUCKING SCARED.

SO I PUT UP WITH MY STUPID GLASSES,
BIDED MY TIME, AND JUST WAITED.
KEEPING A CLOSE EYE ON THE TECHNOLOGY,
WHILE I CONSTANTLY DEBATED.

AND BY THE TIME THE PROCEDURE PROVED SUITABLY STABLE,
IT WAS TOO FUCKING LATE.
AS MY EYES WERE DANGEROUSLY DEGRADED,
AND I WAS STUCK WITH MY SHORT-SIGHTED FATE!

BAT EAR

NOW, BEFORE YOU GO REACHING FOR *GOOGLE*,
I CAN ASSURE YOU I'M NOT MAKING THIS UP.
AS THIS IS A GENUINE MEDICAL CONDITION
THAT CAN'T BE CORRECTED UNTIL YOU'RE A PUP.

AND WHEN I SAY PUP,
I MEAN YOU HAVE TO BE AT LEAST SIX.
SO THE EAR CARTILAGE HAS STOPPED FORMING,
AND CAN TAKE THE SURGICAL FIX.

AND YOU'D HAVE THE CORRECTIVE SURGERY, OF COURSE,
THERE'S NO DOUBT ABOUT THAT.
SO YOU DIDN'T GROW UP WITH TWO EARS,
WHICH MADE YOU RESEMBLE A BAT.

AND ALTHOUGH A LIFETIME OF BEING CALLED *BATMAN*
MIGHT SEEM PRETTY DAMN COOL.
PEOPLE WOULD THINK UP OTHER NAMES
THAT'D BE MUCH MORE HURTFUL AND CRUEL.

AND AS LONG AS THE SURGERY WAS SUCCESSFUL,
THEN FUTURE PEOPLE WOULD NEVER KNOW.
THAT YOU WERE BORN WITH A RARE DEFECT,
WHICH DEALT YOUR LOOKS SUCH A BLOW.

AND YOU MAY THINK THAT ME RHYMING ABOUT THIS SUBJECT
IS BEING EXTREMELY UNKIND.
BUT MY SENSE OF HUMOUR'S FAR TOO DARK AND WARPED
TO PASS UP SUCH A BIZARRE AND AMUSING FIND!

Trainee Doctor:

Raj was a young trainee doctor from Lahore
who unfortunately drew the short straw.
    He had to treat an old lady sleeping rough
    who had open sores and dandruff
and droopy tits that dragged on the floor.

FOOD POISONING

WE GET THIS FROM EATING CONTAMINATED FOOD
FILLED WITH LOTS OF HARMFUL BACTERIA.
AND WE CAN PICK IT UP AT HOME,
OR IN ANY RESTAURANT OR SCHOOL CAFETERIA.

AND COMING UP WITH THOSE TWO LINES WASN'T EASY,
SO I HOPE THEY MADE YOU SMILE.
AND DESPITE WHAT YOU MAY THINK,
THESE RHYMES CAN BE DIFFICULT TO COMPILE.

SO LET'S GET BACK TO THE FOOD POISONING,
WHICH WON'T GIVE US ANY THRILLS.
BUT IT WILL GIVE US VOMITING, DIARRHOEA, CRAMPS,
AND SOME NASTY, FREEZING CHILLS.

IT'LL ALSO TAKE AWAY OUR ENERGY AND APPETITE,
AND GIVE US PLENTY OF MUSCLES ACHES.
AND WE'LL BE CONTINUALLY TOSSING OUR COOKIES,
AND BLOWING CHUNKS FOR AS LONG AS IT TAKES.

AND AS FOR THE BUGS THAT CAUSE IT,
I'M SURE YOU'VE HEARD OF SALMONELLA.
BUT COMPARED TO SOME OF THE OTHERS,
HE'S A FAIRLY MILD SORT OF A FELLA.

SO THE OTHERS ARE FAR MORE AWFUL
SUCH AS, THE NOROVIRUS AND E-COLI.
AS THEY'LL HAVE US PUKING UP OUR STOMACH LININGS,
AND PLEADING TO DIE.

BUT THESE BACTERIA ARE EASY TO AVOID, THOUGH,
SO IF YOU DON'T WANT TO BE STRICKEN.
JUST COOK YOUR FOOD PROPERLY,
ESPECIALLY THE READY-TO-EAT MEALS, EGGS AND CHICKEN!

Famous Food Critic:

There was a famous food critic named Adele
who unfortunately lost her sense of smell.
    This soon cost the poor woman her job,
    'cos when she put food in her gob,
she was fucked-over by her taste buds, as well.

SLOW WALKERS

HATE SEEMS LIKE FAR TOO STRONG A WORD
TO EXPRESS HOW I FEEL ABOUT THIS GROUP.
BUT COMING UP WITH A MORE SUITABLE TERM
IS THROWING ME FOR A LOOP.

SO I'M GOING TO FORGET ABOUT IT FOR NOW,
AND COME BACK TO IT LATER.
ESPECIALLY AS I HAVE NO REAL IDEA
WHETHER OR NOT YOU'RE A PATIENT WAITER.

SO I'M A VERY BRISK WALKER,
AND ALWAYS SET A FURIOUS PACE.
HELL, LET'S BE HONEST,
I PRACTICALLY RUN FROM PLACE TO PLACE.

AND THIS PRESENTS ME WITH AN ANNOYING PROBLEM
ALMOST EVERY SINGLE DAY.
BECAUSE I ENCOUNTER SO MANY SLOW WALKERS
WHO GET IN MY BLOODY WAY.

AND I JUST WANT TO GET WHERE I'M GOING
AS FAST AS I CAN.
WHILE OTHERS LIKE TO STOP AND CHAT,
AND EVEN BARGAIN SCAN.

AND I REALISE THAT PEOPLE NEED TO CATCH-UP,
AND DO SOME WINDOW SHOPPING.
BUT I WANT TO GET TO MY SODDING DESTINATION
WITHOUT ACTUALLY STOPPING.

SO I HAVE TO DODGE AND WEAVE MY WAY THROUGH
ALL THE PEOPLE WHO MEANDER.
AS WELL AS TRYING NOT TO BUMP INTO
THOSE WHO RANDOMLY STOP JUST TO GANDER.

BUT THERE'S NOTHING I CAN DO, OF COURSE,
ABOUT THE SLOW-PACED URBAN EBB AND FLOW.
WHICH IS WHY I DESPISE ALL THOSE PEOPLE
WHO ALWAYS WALK TOO FUCKING SLOW!

5ᴘ BAG TAX

SO, I'VE GOT ONE MORE ANGRY RHYME TO WRITE
BEFORE I CAN FINALLY RELAX.
WHICH REVOLVES AROUND MY BURNING HATRED
OF THE NEW 5ᴘ BAG TAX.

AND I KNOW THE GOVERNMENT DOESN'T GET THE MONEY,
SO IT'S ACTUALLY A CHARGE.
AS WELL AS BEING PERFECTLY AWARE THAT THE SUM OF 5ᴘ
ISN'T ALL THAT VERY LARGE.

AND I ALSO KNOW THAT ALL THE STORES
ARE GOING TO DONATE THE MONEY TO CHARITY.
BUT EVEN THIS PLEASING LITTLE FACT
DOESN'T FULLY RESTORE MY INNER PARITY.

AND NOT EVEN THE SIDE EFFECT
THAT IT'LL HELP TO REDUCE LITTER.
IS GOING TO PIERCE MY STONY HEART,
AND MAKE ME ANY LESS BITTER.

AND OTHER COUNTRIES, OF COURSE,
HAVE BEEN DOING THIS FOR YEARS.
SO WE'RE ONE OF THE LAST NATIONS
TO ACTUALLY SWITCH GEARS.

AND I USED THE PLASTIC BAGS
TO COLLECT RUBBISH IN THE KITCHEN.
BUT EVEN THIS TERRIBLE LOSS
DOESN'T ACCOUNT FOR MY BITCHIN'.

AND I GET PEOPLE WANTING TO SAVE THE PLANET,
EVEN THOUGH IT'S FAR TOO LATE.
SO IT ISN'T EVEN THIS NAIVETY
THAT'S MAKING ME IRATE.

NO, THE REAL REASON I'M UPSET
BY THE INTRODUCTION OF THIS SMALL FEE.
IS SIMPLY THE FACT THAT I'M BEING ASKED TO PAY
FOR SOMETHING THAT'S ALWAYS BEEN FREE!

PICKUP LINES

I STILL LOVE A GREAT PICKUP LINE,
EVEN THOUGH I DON'T USE THEM ANYMORE.
SO LET'S COVER SOME OF MY FAVOURITES, THEN,
LIKE, *YOUR DRESS WOULD LOOK GREAT ON MY FLOOR.*

AND I LIKED TO KEEP THINGS FUN.
AND I LIKED TO PLAY THE JOKER.
SO I'D GIVE A GIRL A CHEEKY GRIN AND ASK
DO YOU KNOW HOW TO PLAY STRIP POKER?

AND THIS ONE'S A REAL CLASSIC.
IT'S STRAIGHT OUT OF MY ALL-TIME TOP SEVEN.
JUST LOOK CONCERNED AND THEN ASK
DID IT HURT WHEN YOU FELL FROM HEAVEN?

BUT IF CLASSIC DOESN'T DO THE TRICK,
THEN HERE'S ONE FROM MY WEIRD TOP TEN.
DO YOU HAVE ANY RAISINS?
NO? HOW ABOUT A DATE, THEN?

AND WHILE WEIRD CHATUP LINES ARE OK,
YOU NEED TO AVOID BEING CREEPY.
SO BE CAREFUL USING, *IF I FOLLOWED YOU HOME,*
WOULD YOU KEEP ME?

BUT DO TRY, *IF YOU COOK ME BREAKFAST,*
THEN I'LL COOK YOU DINNER.
THOUGH, YOU MIGHT WANT TO REARRANGE THE PHRASES
IN ORDER TO DELIVER A WINNER.

AND YOU'LL NEED TO PICK THE RIGHT LADY,
SO THAT UNAMUSED DRINKS DON'T GET HURLED.
BEFORE YOU TRY, *ARE YOU FROM OUTER SPACE, GIRL?*
'COS YOUR ARSE IS OUT OF THIS WORLD.

AND IF YOU SURVIVE THAT, MY FRIEND,
AND SHE HASN'T TORN OFF YOUR HEAD.
THEN YOU COULD TRY, *I'VE LOST MY TEDDY BEAR.*
CAN I HUG YOU, INSTEAD?

BUT IF NONE OF THAT STUFF WORKS, THOUGH,
THEN ONLY SHOCK TACTICS WILL SUFFICE.
SO SHOUT, *FAT POLAR BEAR!*
WHAT?
I JUST WANTED TO SAY SOMETHING TO BREAK THE ICE.

AND IF THAT DOESN'T GET A GIRL'S ATTENTION,
THEN YOU COULD TRY CHANNELLING THE *HOFF.*
AND FINALLY, *THERE'S A HUGE SALE IN MY BEDROOM.*
CLOTHES ARE 100% OFF!

BAD JOKES

I ONLY REMEMBER BAD JOKES, UNFORTUNATELY;
NEVER JOKES THAT ARE FUN.
GUESS WHO I BUMPED INTO AT THE OPTICIANS RECENTLY?
EVERYONE...

AND NOW THAT I'VE SHARED THAT TERRIBLE JOKE,
YOU CAN UNDERSTAND MY PLIGHT.
WHAT DO YOU GET IF YOU CROSS A SNOWMAN WITH A VAMPIRE?
SERIOUS FROSTBITE.

AND IT'S LIKE THE GOOD JOKE ALWAYS VANISHES,
BUT THE TERRIBLE ONE LINGERS.
WHY DO GORILLAS HAVE BIG NOSTRILS?
BECAUSE THEY HAVE BIG FINGERS.

AND ONCE THE BAD JOKE IS STUCK,
IT SIMPLY BECOMES ENGRAVED.
WHAT DID ONE OCEAN SAY TO THE OTHER OCEAN?
NOTHING, THEY JUST WAVED.

AND I DON'T GET WHY THIS HAPPENS TO ME.
IT DOESN'T MAKE ANY SENSE.
DID YOU HEAR ABOUT THE CIRCUS FIRE?
IT WAS INTENSE...

AND IT'S BECOME SO BAD LATELY,
THAT I DON'T KNOW WHAT TO DO.
TWO CANNIBALS EATING A CLOWN...
...DOES THIS TASTE FUNNY TO YOU?

AND I NEVER HEAR ANY LAUGHS, OF COURSE,
JUST LOTS OF FRUSTRATED GROANS.
WHAT DO PRISONERS USE TO CALL EACH OTHER?
THEY USE THEIR CELL PHONES.

AND I'D LOVE TO REMEMBER A GOOD JOKE.
IT'S MY DEAREST WISH.
WHY WOULDN'T THE LOBSTER SHARE HIS TOYS?
BECAUSE HE WAS SHELLFISH.

SO, WE'VE REACHED THE END OF THIS RHYME,
AND THE END OF THE BOOK.
AND I HOPE YOU FOUND IT FUNNY, MY FRIEND,
AND WELL-WORTH ANOTHER LOOK.

AND I'LL LEAVE YOU WITH ONE FINAL BAD JOKE,
JUST TO BE A PAIN IN THE NECK.
WHAT LIES TWITCHING AT THE BOTTOM OF THE OCEAN?
A NERVOUS FUCKING WRECK!

THE END

ABOUT THE AUTHOR

JON THOMAS is basically one of those people who generally speaks without thinking first, so he tends to say whatever comes into his head, which has, on occasion, had the effect of reducing a small roomful of people to hysterical tears without him really understanding why.

And with that in mind, Jon has decided to share his strange sense of humour with the world using the fun medium of rhyme in the hope that it makes people laugh, cry, and even occasionally wet themselves. Or, at the very least, it cheers them up a little bit after a crappy day at work!

Jon would also like to thank you for deciding to purchase this book and would greatly appreciate you leaving a review if you enjoyed reading it and the loosely related bonus limericks.

ALSO BY JON THOMAS

PAPERBACKS

GUYS AND GALS

100 FUNNY & RUDE RHYMES FOR COUPLES

MIXED BAG

200 FUNNY & RUDE LIMERICKS, RHYMES & IRATE MONOLOGUES

CHEAP LAUGHS

150 FUNNY & RUDE RHYMES FOR ADULTS ONLY

KINDLE BOOKS

BOOKS OF RHYME

LIFE

A CLUTCH OF 50 MOSTLY FUN RHYMES

SICK

A BOWL OF 50 UNWELL FUN RHYMES

EAT, SLEEP, RHYME, REPEAT
A CHAOTIC COLLECTION OF 50 RANDOM FUN RHYMES

RANT
A SEETHING COLLECTION OF 50 ANGRY FUN RHYMES

2015
A NEWSWORTHY COLLECTION OF 50 TOPICAL FUN RHYMES

RAVE
A JOYFUL COLLECTION OF 50 HAPPY FUN RHYMES

GUYS
50 THINGS THAT WOMEN NEED TO REALISE ABOUT MEN

GALS
50 THINGS THAT MEN NEED TO REALISE ABOUT WOMEN

POT LUCK
A CRAZY COLLECTION OF 50 RANDOM FUN RHYMES

PURE GOLD
A WITTY COMPILATION OF MY 50 MOST FUN RHYMES

WOOF

(IT'S A DOG'S LIFE)
50 FUNNY AND RUDE RHYMES FOR DOG OWNERS

BOOKS OF POETRY

WILD

50 DESCRIPTIVE ANIMAL POEMS

BOOKS OF IRATE MONOLOGUES

PURE RAGE

AN IRRATIONAL COLLECTION OF 25 FUN IRATE MONOLOGUES

SHORT STORIES

2067

THE EXTINCTION OF THE HUMAN RACE

DRAGONS DAWN

THE REAL HISTORY OF DRAGONS

BOOKS OF LIMERICKS

WTF!

100 FUNNY & RUDE LIMERICKS FOR ADULTS

OMG!

100 FUNNY & RUDE LIMERICKS FOR ADULTS

LOL!

100 FUNNY & RUDE LIMERICKS FOR ADULTS

SSDD

100 FUNNY & RUDE LIMERICKS FOR ADULTS

TFIF

100 FUNNY & RUDE LIMERICKS FOR ADULTS

NSFW

100 FUNNY & RUDE LIMERICKS FOR ADULTS

Main cover image care of: © Ron Leishman Toonaday.com

Comments are welcome via email at:
jonny.e.thomas@gmail.com